LOSS OF INNOCENCE

A VIETNAM WAR STORY

By

Larry Murley

Illustrations by Kerry Kelly

ISBN-10: 0996014802
ISBN-13: 978-0-9960148-0-9

DEDICATION

To all the Montagnard people who allied with the American Forces in the Vietnam War and have lost their homes, their families, or their lives.

For early pictures and stories of Vietnam, for links to You Tube videos and stories by other Vietnam vets, we welcome you to join us on our Facebook page at
http://www.facebook.com/lossofinnocence

FOREWORD

This story is written to tell of the beginnings of one of America's most controversial conflicts - the Vietnam War.

Vietnam was a country that had seen war for generations in one form or another, a country that had lived in constant subjugation. We, the USA, have positioned people there for years, long before the period in which this story takes place. I felt moved to tell this, not just as a story full blown, but to perhaps arouse the interests of our young people, our students. With the amount of information available on the internet and in printed form, and with the stories written and published by the Veterans themselves, they might be able to know the truth about this piece of our country's history, and avoid its mistakes at a later time. We started Vietnam with CIA and Special Forces leading out, then an escalation of personnel, and the greater cost that it led to, both in lives and injuries, and funding. Afghanistan, in our present time, had the same birth, and has come to the same end.

Our country will always have enemies and those who wish to cause us harm. But we need to find another way to defend ourselves. Boots on the ground is not the answer anymore. You can't fight an enemy in his front yard, he will always win. He can out wait you. His resources are there, you have to transport yours. Your soldiers' thoughts and dreams are back at home, his are right there with him. You are not a part of them. Even our leaders are not sure what to do about Afghanistan, Syria, North Korea and probably a few other spots around the globe. Half of our countries resources are spent in this useless enterprise. We need to start thinking out of the box. Some say being an isolationist is not the answer. No, it isn't. Forget about that. I won't go forward and spout my solutions. Opinions are like assholes - everyone has one, and few people want to look at someone else's.

I feel that knowledge of history, and not repeating it, is the best answer and making ourselves strong, not only physically, but technologically and scientifically. But then, that is just my opinion, and we have discussed that.

Oh, yeah, I have asked that this book be printed in large type. I feel there will be a lot of old Coots and Cootesses' that will want to read it. I have found that in my later years that things have gotten too small, I would rather you be able to read this without squinting.

The book is written as fiction, but I think there are a lot of truths in it. A lot of the people didn't exist, but others like them most certainly did. I, as the author, was able to see a beautiful Vietnam before we destroyed it. I liked some of the people, and loved some of the others. My time there was very short compared to some, but it was enough to make a lasting impression on me. Do I want to return? No, I don't. It would not be the same. I prefer to see it as it was in my memories. The day I flew out of Da Nang, May 12, 1962.

Larry Murley

CHAPTER 1

Saigon in 1961 was a big city even then. I always enjoyed walking down Tu Do Street late in the afternoon or early evening. Sometimes I would sit in the sidewalk cafe at the Continental Hotel and watch the people, especially the beautiful girls in their beautiful, flowing dresses riding their bicycles. Sometimes I would watch a movie in a theater down the street. . It was surprisingly cool on the shaded streets even in the muggy tropical air. I found that the streets looked surprisingly like the French Quarter in New Orleans, Louisiana, due to its French influence.

I had been doing some training with my group in Nigeria for about a month when one morning the CO came in to breakfast and said, "OK guys, finish eating. Get your gear together and saddle up. We are leaving immediately."

A few hours later we were airborne somewhere over Africa. I was sitting in my seat when the 1st Sgt. walked by. I couldn't help asking, "Hey Sarge! Where we going?"

He turned and looked at me like only a top non-com can look at you.

"Son, you are going to Vietnam."

I looked at him a minute. "Sarge, where in fuck is Vietnam?"

He smiled and said, "Son, it's a vacation spot over in Southeast Asia!"

Yeah, right!

Now here I am. We landed at Tan Son Nhut Air Base about 11:30 in the morning local time. I stepped off that plane and immediately every particle of clothing was wet! Oh my God! I thought Africa was hot. I thought Arizona was hot. But this was the most miserable place on Earth. What in hell would the USA want with this place? The officer at the bottom of the boarding ramp announced, "Load up on that truck over there! You are going to be briefed!"

A short, sticky, smothering, hot ride later we arrived at a hanger converted into a command center. We were seated. At least it was 20 degrees cooler than outside. After a few minutes a handful of brass arrived. A red faced major stood up and spoke.

"Gentlemen, welcome to Viet-Nam! We hope your stay here will be as pleasant as possible. However, Captain - let us say Allen here - will brief you on the do's and don'ts of this fine place. Captain?"

"Gentlemen, let me start with your immediate surroundings. Firstly, due to the climate here it is extremely important that you keep your canteens filled and drink plenty of water, but only from the potable water containers at the base. Do not drink water from the city or any of the towns and villages you may visit. As for showering, you must do your showering with an allotment of 1 gallon of water. Basically wet down, soap up, and rinse off and hope you get it all, lest you break out in skin irritations. Do not brush your teeth with the shower water. I repeat, do not!

"Now, how many of you are married or have girlfriends back home that you care about? Show of hands please!"

A smattering of hands went up.

"OK, you will be allowed liberties and passes to go into Saigon. Gentlemen, this is a dangerous place for many reasons. My advice to you is keep your pants zipped. If you are too weak, then wear at least 2 condoms. Gentlemen, this old city has venereal diseases that we not only can't treat, we don't even know what they are. We have hospital addresses you can visit if you don't believe me. Secondly, don't go into town alone. Buddy up. Don't let anything get you off onto side streets. Stay alert. There is a price on your head. You may make friends with a local man or woman and get very close and find out that they are Viet-Cong. They are the enemy, in case you haven't heard, and they don't wear ID cards.

"Secondly, when you go into the country, beware that we have at least 2 of the most poisonous snakes in the world here. The Cobra, and the Blue Krait. Both are deadly. Find out what they look like, what their habits are. There are also lethal insects here. Most of you are going to be living with them, so prepare yourself. Also, there are tigers in the jungle. They will hunt you, they will kill you, and they will eat you. Have a good visit, gentlemen!"

Yeah, a great vacation spot!

The Captain continued. "Next, you should know that although you are still a part of the US military, the operation here in Vietnam is under CIA supervision. They give the orders. You will get your assignments tomorrow. You will be taken over to tent city for the evening. Dinner is served in the big hanger just up the road, breakfast, too. Everyone report here 0700 hours tomorrow. Good afternoon."

The first shower was less than enjoyable. Dinner was quite good. Indeed better than most military food. The tents held eight men. They were screened and had rough hewn wood flooring. I later found out the wood was solid mahogany. Imagine that. I had grown up cutting wood for winter heat and cooking all my young life. I knew what mahogany was. I had seen tables and furniture made of it that were very expensive. Here, it was just rough cut flooring.

After dinner I walked around the base a bit. In the middle of tent city was the remains of what looked like an old temple of sorts with a short wall along one side. I crawled up on it and sat down, nervously looking around for some of those funny sounding snakes. The sun set as I sat on that wall and smoked a Chesterfield King, and contemplated my first day in Vietnam

I wandered back to the big hanger that

housed a kitchen, mess hall, library, barbershop, a PX, and Post Office, and became a movie theater after dark. I don't remember what was playing that night, but needless to say it was not a first screening.

Next morning, after a good breakfast at the all-included hanger, I walked to the briefing room from yesterday. Several of the same people from the day before were already there and more were arriving. I said a few hellos to ones that I knew, but my eyes were drawn to a single person seated at the rear of the room. He was dressed in khaki pants and a short, outside-the-trousers blue sports shirt. He wore a straw beer drinking hat. You know the type - a round, kinda rolled up brim with buttons 'round in various places. He was probably 5 feet 9 inches or so tall, maybe 165 lbs, and had absolutely no military look whatsoever. I thought, "What a strange person." About that time someone touched my sleeve.

"Would you come with me?"

"Yes, Sir" I answered.

He was another non-uniformed man in his early 30's. Reminded me of the bookkeeper at the local grain elevator back home. I followed him down a long hallway past several cubicles and into a small room. He motioned for me to sit down across from the only desk in the room. He reached out his hand and smiled,

"My name is Dan. Forget the rest; you may never see me again.

"You have been chosen for an assignment for the next few weeks. I would like to ask you a few questions."

I nodded, "Yes, Sir."

"First of all, you grew up in a very rural area and did a lot of hunting, even early in your life."

"Yes, sir. Hunting was a big part of supplying food for our table."

"You had a religious upbringing."

I frowned. "Yes, sir."

"Are you still religious?"

"I suppose so, sir. I believe in God, if that's what you mean."

"OK. What if someone ordered you to kill someone?"

"Well, sir, when I entered the military I kinda knew it might happen sometime."

"Could you do it?"

"Yes sir, I think so!"

"Ok. From this moment on everything I say to you, you will never be able to repeat. When you leave here you will be taken to Saigon. You will first be taken back to get your gear. At that time you will change into civilian clothes. All military clothing will be picked up and stored for you. All military ID cards and dog tags will be surrendered; any pictures of family or letters will also be surrendered. These will be kept and returned at a later date. Do you understand?"

A very puzzled "Yes, sir" escaped my lips. Holy Shit!

"Now, let me introduce your new partner, and I will leave you in his capable hands."

At that moment the man from the back of the room walked in, and reached out his hand.

"Hi, I'm Silver. No", he said, as I started to reply. "I don't want to know who you are. We will come up with something later."

"OK. Ok, sir."

"Well, don't call me 'Sir'. I am not a fucking Officer or a Fucking Gentleman either!"

A couple of hours later found me all dressed in jeans and a western shirt, my favorite pair of Nocona boots, and with my two inch wide leather belt and silver buckle, checking into the Continental Hotel in downtown Saigon with a brand new name and the credentials to go with it. My neighbor was my newfound friend, known only as Silver. I quickly unpacked my meager belongings and put them away. I walked out on my balcony and my gaze fell to the street below. *What a beautiful city,* I thought. The sounds and smells were like nowhere I had ever been. I was quite anxious to explore my new surroundings. The thought had no sooner occupied my mind than a sharp knock was at my door. It was Silver.

"Are you ready to go see Saigon?"

"You read my mind," was my reply.

Ok, you have made it this far. Soon my story is going to get more serious. The first chapter or so you may not like. That's ok. I didn't like it either. It went against everything that I was made of in my life. It is necessary to write it to make sense of the things to come, and who I would become. During this period of my life, the coming events would prove to influence me all of my days. So be patient, and try to understand how any young man can be changed by the environment that he is thrust into, and must survive in, if he is to live!

We went downstairs and out to the tables on the sidewalk near the entrance, down the Tu Do Street side, and took a seat. The early evening breeze coming up the street off the water was cooling, and made for a pleasant comfortable surrounding. The other side of the entrance of the Continental was facing the Government of South Vietnam building. An impressive building, but not as pleasant a view as the one we had. On the other side of Tu Do Street were rows of small shops selling clothing, jewelry, and whatever one might imagine for the locality.

Silver spoke, "Would you like me to order you some dinner? Would you like French or Vietnamese?"

I thought for a moment. "Hell, how about Vietnamese. I am in the country for a while, might as well go native."

Silver grinned. "Good choice."

We sat and chatted and smoked a cigarette while watching the tiny Renault-Dauphine taxis and the bicycle rickshaws with the seats out in front of the rider peddling rider.

Silver laughed and said, "If you have an accident you are the first one there!"

"Makes me nervous," I said. We watched the traffic. As the streets all intersected from four directions with no lights, or other traffic control, it was just a melting pot of cars, scooters, bicycles and rickshaws. But I don't think I ever saw an accident. Our food came in courses. A soup of indistinguishable origin, slightly spicy, but delicious. Then some greens and vegetables wrapped in a thin rice paper and dipped into a sauce that Silver warned me about. "Don't smell that stuff, or you will never use it. Just use it sparingly and it's really good." Boy, was he right! It was made from fish, and it smelled like it! There was a plate of rice and chicken, and we finished with a crème desert of some kind. It was an awesome meal. I wiped my mouth on a napkin and sat back and lit another Chesterfield King. "I could get used to this,

Mr. Silver!"

"Mister? Anyway, enjoy it while you can. You won't be here forever."

Ok, now is the time to ask him, I thought. "Silver," I asked, "what is all this about? There is nothing in the uniform code of military conduct that covers circumstances like this. That I can find anyway."

"Well, 'Mister'. We will find out in a few days. I was told we will be briefed shortly. Until then we are just two tourists, out enjoying *The Pearl of the Orient*! Ok, let's go exploring!"

As we walked down Tu Do Street toward the river, my eyes and ears were full of sights and sounds. We caught a boat across to Cho'Lon. When we got there I remembered this place is off-limits to military personnel. I whispered this to Silver. He looked at me, "I don't see no dog tags on you." Oh right, I forgot! For hours we wandered in and out of the bars and various other establishments, keeping quietly to ourselves, watching the people. About 2200 hours we caught another boat back and walked back to our hotel. Sleep did not come easy that night. Questions filled my head and the circumstances of the day puzzled me greatly. Next morning, seeing no sign of Silver, I walked across Tu Do Street and up the street. Soon I found myself in this huge open market with fruits and vegetables the like of which I never knew existed. The smells were overpowering, literally. I had exchanged a few dollars for some Vietnamese Dong, so if something looked enticing I would sample it. And that is the way I had my breakfast on my third day in Vietnam. Soon I worked my way back to the hotel and ordered a glass of tea and was enjoying it, watching three beautiful Vietnamese girls in their white Au Dias, talking and laughing to themselves. *My God! They sounded like songbirds!*

"G'morning, Boots. I figured I would find you out here. Been up long?"

"Not long. Had breakfast in the market."

Silver frowned slightly. "Exploring, huh? Be careful. This place is beautiful, but it can be dangerous for a person alone. Boots! Yeah, it fits. All I ever see you wear are those fancy cowboy boots. So, Boots it is!

"So, Boots, have you ever done much fighting?" The question amused me. I had been brought up in a household of peaceful people. Fighting had never been encouraged.

"Nope, other than normal schoolyard scrapes as a kid. Why?"

"Well, I need to teach you a little bit of hand to hand. It might come in handy."

"Ok." I answered.

After lunch we caught a taxi to the Embassy compound. As we arrived, my first thought was *Here is a little bit of America in an alien setting.* Everyone seemed busy, mostly pleasant, but not incredibly friendly though! Silver lead me out to a small, grassy garden area. It was slightly more private than the main building. We changed into some gym shoes and walked out in the middle of the garden and stood facing each other. I was about 2 or 3 inches taller, probably 35 pounds heavier, and had a much longer reach. I was pretty confident I could take care of myself.

Silver spoke. "What I am going to teach you is an oriental type of self defense. It is much different than probably anything you have been exposed to, so go ahead and throw a punch at me. Give it your best shot!"

I did not like this immediately, and he saw the puzzled look that was probably dripping off my face. "Come on now, this is necessary". Ok, I pulled myself into what I thought would be my best boxing stance, and made a sharp left jab at his face. I found myself flying by him off-balance and half falling. He had simply deflected my jab and sidestepped me, using my momentum to send me flying past him.

"Try again," he said.

This time I charged him with a right hook. About the time it should have landed, I felt myself being lifted by my right shoulder and arm and I went sailing over him and landed on my back. That pissed me off. I was up in an instant and charged for his midsection to get him down and maybe do some payback stuff. Anyway, it wasn't a very thought out move, because moments later I was trimming the grass with my teeth. I didn't get up so fast that time.

"Sorry for being so rough on you, but I had to make a point. Oriental fighting is much different. You learn to use your opponent's strength against him. Now, you're ready to learn."

"Yes, Sir" I remarked, still slightly peeved.

"You better watch that 'Sir' shit," he frowned, "or you will piss me off!"

The rest of the day was spent learning how to punch and kick and do it all while keeping your balance and staying focused at the same time. That evening he told me about studying the martial arts and learning the philosophy behind them, and about meditating for hours with his teachers. Some of it sounded interesting, and some sounded very strange. This new partner of mine was a very complex man. He was a bit older than I thought at first, being in his late thirties. He had been in the military, and out and in again, since he was 16. He had lied about his age and had entered WWII and had survived the Pacific battles. Then he left the military, but couldn't find his way in the civilian world. He re-entered , served in Korea, and had remained in Southeast Asia. He had been in Laos, and had already been in Vietnam for some time.

The next morning as we had breakfast Silver asked, "Can you shoot?"

I looked at him "I am considerably better at that than I am at hand fighting."

He laughed. "Good. Let's go see."

A couple of hours later found us at a military firing range out near Tan Son Nuht military base. We fired a couple of 45's a few times, switched over to a couple of M2 carbines and fired them both singly and on full automatic. Silver went into the ammo shack and came back with a rifle. I recognized it immediately as a 1903 model Springfield 30-06.

"Here," he said, "try some long shots."

I took the rifle. I had always loved the feel of it, and had deer hunted with one. I took a rest on some sand bags, picked a target out at about 200 yards. I rested, let out my breath, and squeezed the trigger. I levered another round into the chamber, repeated the process, and squeezed. After the third round Silver said, "Let's go see how you did."

We walked down to the target and found I had hit within 4 inches of the center all three times.

"Huh!" said Silver. "With a little practice you might do alright."

"Hey! That would have been meat on the

table."

"Boots, we're not hunting for dinner."

Oh, yeah, now I remember. I was silent and thoughtful for some time afterward.

Later that evening we walked down the street to a dive - a bar I suppose. Although I noticed a lot of traffic up and down the back stairway of pretty girls and the male patrons, I also noticed a guy that I had flown in with, sitting at one of the tables. I told Silver that I was going to go visit with him. He said ok, so I went over and fell into a conversation with Ronnie and a couple of his friends. Silver sat down on a stool at the bar, and immediately one of the pretty Vietnamese girls slithered up and hung herself on his arm. I smiled. Before long we were also joined by female company wanting the Number One GI's to buy the Number 10 girls a drink. My conservative background just balked at that idea for some reason. But it wasn't a problem, because the rest of the guys didn't have a problem with it. So an atmosphere of merriment soon prevailed.

Some hours later Silver appeared to be in earnest conversation with the girl. He seemed to be able to converse in

Vietnamese quite well. About then, three US sailors barged through the wide doorway, loudly letting the world know the Navy had arrived or something like that. After surveying the room, the biggest toughest one made a beeline to Silver and his girl. Taking her by the arm, he warmly welcomed her to join him and his buddies. She pulled her arm free and told him 'NO' in very good English, that she was busy. This did not deter the determined sailor. He once again attempted to assist her in changing partners. Once again she resisted. At this point Silver turned halfway on his stool and remarked to the sailor that the young lady had said no and perhaps he should look around for other company. At this the sailor drew himself up, swaggered over, and presented himself in Silver's face. Literally. I think somehow this was what he was looking for anyway. Someone to bully.

He said to Silver, "Look little man. Maybe *you* should just keep your trap shut!"

Silver smiled, "I was, until you disrupted the young lady and myself!"

"Yeah, well, go find yourself another whore, I want this one."

Silver's smile narrowed. "Now that's not

going to happen. I would like you to back up some, I don't like the odor of what you have drinking in my face."

At that the sailor backed slightly. I saw the punch coming but it never landed. The man just kinda expelled a huge breath of air and crumpled. At that his two mates moved into the foray but they didn't seem to be able to land any blows either. In a few seconds Silver, all by himself, had put them out onto the sidewalk. And he hadn't even lost his little straw beer-drinking hat.

"Dammit, Silver! I was gonna help." I exclaimed.

"Yeah, too bad, it was turning into a good evening, . Let's go before they come back with half the Navy."

Next morning as we were having breakfast, Dan, the guy from my first day, abruptly sat down at our table saying, "Mind if I join you?"

We grunted our approval while chewing our food. His next question was directed at me, but Silver interjected, "Just call him 'Boots'."

Dan smiled. "Morning, Boots. Gentlemen, hope you have been enjoying your vacation, but now it's time to go to work." I watched Silver's face as seriousness walked across it, and something inside me seemed to take an ominous direction. But, oh well, it was never supposed to be walk in the park.

Dan handed Silver a piece of paper. "The man I have mentioned here has been confirmed to be a traitor to the Republic of South Vietnam. He must be neutralized by whatever means possible. This is your job. It should be sooner than later, however, and it should be done as covertly as possible, in a way as to not bring embarrassment to the government or President Ngo Dinh Diem.

You will be furnished with whatever you need. Look him up, scout him out, and in a couple of days a Vietnamese man will approach you and ask if you need any special foods. Give him a list, and whatever you need will be delivered. Dan stood, and as he turned to leave, smiled and said " Good morning, gentlemen, enjoy your breakfast!"

My thoughts were *Sorry, Dan, you pretty much screwed that up and it was a good breakfast!*

After breakfast we returned to Silver's room and opened the envelope that Dan had given us. Inside were a couple of pieces of paper and a picture of a Vietnamese gentleman in his mid to late 40's. He was well-groomed and nicely dressed in a white suit. He appeared to have no distinguishing appearances We both read the information that we were given about him. For the sake of a name let us call him 'Quang'. We had his address at home and his office address, which just happened to be in the building around the corner from our hotel. We were given a few other bits of info about him.

I got up and walked to the window that looked out over the entrance to the government building. "We should be able to see him from here."

"We need to get better acquainted than that."

I thought to myself, and then said out loud, "You're the boss. You obviously have done this before."

Silver looked at me, and said almost to satisfy my mind, "Don't think too much about it. It is just like any other job. You plan it out and go do it carefully and thoughtfully and it will come out ok."

"Ok," I said.

The next few days were spent watching the actions and daily routines of Mr. Quang. He seemed to have a great many friends, but no immediate family surfaced. No wife, no children. He traveled in a wide social circle in public and a much narrower one in private. Occasionally, he would go to Cho'Lon and frequented an establishment that was both a brothel and a gambling den - a hangout for some very shady characters.

About a week after Dan had approached us Silver came to my room one evening.

"Boots, I have a plan,"

"Ok, tell me." I responded.

"Tomorrow night we are going for a boat ride. Maybe shoot some ducks."

I didn't really think for a minute he was referring to real ducks. Next evening after dinner I went upstairs to find a few items of clothing on my bed.

Silver said "Pick something, get dressed, and come next door."

A few minutes later,I appeared in clothes I

would have never bought for myself: slacks, baggy dark shirt, fedora-type hat, wingtip slippers. Silver looked at me. His only remark was, "I would never have recognized you."

We went down to the street and to a boat dock a short distance down river. A boat with a young Vietnamese man was waiting. We boarded, and a few minutes later we tied up at an abandoned dock a short ways upriver. Silver pulled a tarp in the bow of the boat aside, revealing two rifles with scopes, one of them a Springfield. We stepped onto the dock, taking the rifles with us.

"Boots, look out about two and a half football fields. See the lights of the brothel? You will recognize it as the one we were in a few nights ago. In awhile Quang is going to exit the brothel and get into a boat. We have to get him before he gets into the boat. Check out your weapon."

I picked up the .06 and, laying it on a big crate, I found a position reasonably comfortable. This would not be too easy with bad light and all. I slid the bolt back and watched the long slender cartridge slide into the bore. It seemed almost mechanical. I then looked through the scope and, as the people across the water almost jumped into my view, I realized what I was about to do. Silver's voice reached out of the darkness. "When you see him and get ready, count to three before you pull the trigger. I will back you up".

I watched the crowd for what must have been 30 minutes or so. Then I saw Quang's white suit appear. There were too many people behind him. I was sweating, the water running down into my eyes.

Silver sensed my discomfort. "Take it easy. Relax, pick your shot."

I wiped my eyes, and brought the crosshairs back to the center of Quang's chest. Then, almost as if it was choreographed, everyone moved. He was clear. I breathed my breath out and slowly squeezed the trigger. The rifle recoiled against my shoulder, and Quang disappeared.

Silver said "Good shot, he's down. Let's go."

He took the rifle from me and tossed both it and his own rifle into the river. We climbed back into the boat. We didn't go back to where we started from, but instead we landed someplace else, and a little Dauphine taxi picked us up. About two hours later we were back in our hotel. I sat in my room and suddenly found myself quite ill. I lost my dinner, and maybe even my lunch from the day before. All the pictures in my mind were of my Sunday School teachers, my parents, my grandparents. What would they think? I lay down on my bed, but I don't remember anything after that.

As the sounds of the city brought me back to life the next morning my thoughts went back to the previous evening. The reality settled over me. I wondered about the man I had just killed. Guilt and a kind of illness invaded my thoughts until they were shattered by a knock on the door. I arose and opened the door. Silver was standing there.

"Come on, let's go have breakfast."

"I am not sure I want anything."

He looked at my rumpled sweaty clothing. "Go shower, get dressed. Meet me downstairs."

He turned and walked away. Thirty minutes later I joined him. We ate in silence. As we finished, he wiped his mouth on a napkin and said, "We are going for a ride today."

"Ok," I muttered.

We took a taxi out to Tan Son Nuht and got a jeep and headed north. A little while later a pervasive smell seemed to fill the air. I looked at Silver. He said nothing. A few minutes later we started to see bodies lying alongside the road covered in white lime. Lots'a bodies. And the smell got worse. Soon we arrived at the small military installation at Ben Hoa. We parked the jeep and went inside a tent. Silver led the way. We approached a middle-aged Vietnamese man with graying hair. He wore the insignia of a Captain in the ARVN, Army of Vietnam. He smiled warmly at Silver, and they shook hands.

Silver introduced us, "Meet my friend Boots." I shook hands with the Captain. "Boots, this is Nguyen Than Ngo. Ngo, would you tell Boots about all those bodies back there on the road?"

The Captain looked at me. "Sit please," he said, in very good English. Ngo proceeded to tell me about the young soldiers.

"They had been in a training camp that had been overrun by Viet Cong and had been slaughtered to a man. Most of them were not over 18 years of age. We heard the slaughter, and caught the VC as they were leaving the barracks. We killed almost all of them. Those are their bodies that you saw. We left them there to remind the VC that we are going to remain free men."

Silver turned to me. "Ngo's seventeen year old son was among the young soldiers killed." I looked at the Captain. He showed no expression, but he could not hide the sadness in his eyes.

As we headed back toward Saigon, Silver spoke. "Boots, I know you were having some problems about last night's business."

I looked at him. I didn't think 'business' quite described things.

"I wanted you to know, Quang was responsible for this massacre of the young soldiers, and by taking him out he won't be able to do something like that again."

I thought for a moment. "Tell me why we are doing these things, maybe I can live with myself a little better."

The rest of the ride was somewhat quite,

Silver would sometimes point out something of interest, and I would acknowledge it. I decided that afternoon that this was what I had volunteered for, and as long as I could feel I was doing something good, I would man up to it. My Grandfather Chris had always said, "If you have a job, see to it that you do it good." I had always believed in that. His father had been a Civil War soldier, and had been in some of the worse battles of that period and had survived for over 40 years after it had ended. He had done his duty, and I would do mine!

CHAPTER 2

The next few days were busy with my training. I put all my mind and heart into it; something told me I would need it in the future and I was not wrong. Seems like our breakfast or dinners were always getting interrupted with some "operative" appearing with instructions of some sort. I didn't always have to do the dirty work; Silver took his share of turns. He was always fair with me. One evening we were waiting in a building watching the home of a rich cabinet member in President Diem's cabinet. He was selling secret troop movements to the VC, and they were getting hit hard in every move they made. We knew his wife made frequent trips to North Vietnam. Well, this night I had the gentleman in my crosshairs. We had Silver's backup ready. We always did that, knowing we would only have one chance. I counted 3-2-1, breathed out, and squeezed. As the trigger released, and the rifle bucked, I saw his wife step in front of him. They both went down, the bullet penetrating both of them.

Silver said, "Let's go."

Later, back at the hotel, Silver said "Don't concern yourself. She had ties in North Vietnam. She probably was part of the whole thing anyway." Still, it haunted me for some time. I was brought up to respect and revere women in general.

Later that evening, my dreams were shattered by a knocking on my door. I opened it. Silver was dressed. He said, "Get dressed quickly, we gotta go."

Forty-five minutes later we were on a plane lifting off from Tan Son Nhut airport, myself and Silver and two others I didn't recognize. The guy briefing us, talking loud over the noise, told us about a woman and child being captured by VC somewhere north of Da Nang, with the husband being a high ranking officer in the ARVN. We knew who and where they were, but they were just inside North Vietnam. Our job was to get them out. We were given arms and gear and parachutes, and given our instructions on getting out. In a short time we were over the jump zone, and then stepping out into inky blackness. The rush of wind, the sudden jerk of the chute as it filled with air, it all seemed as if it were a dream, a dream that was becoming reality. I finally found the horizon. I could see others below and above me, and then it got dark. I readied myself for the landing. Then I felt something touch my leg. I touched down, rolled and pulled the chute down. Wow, don't want to do that a lot. I put my whistle to my lips: a short tweet, answered by three more. In minutes we were grouped and moving out. We walked in silence for a couple of hours. I could smell salt water. I knew we must be near the coast.

Dusty, one of the other two men, was walking point. He signaled a stop. We gathered. He told us we had to find cover before daylight. A patch of trees were ahead and off to our right, and I pointed toward them. Dusty nodded. We entered the trees, and each of us found one to climb. We tied ourselves into as comfortable of a position as possible and proceeded to get some sleep, taking turns keeping watch. I awoke around early afternoon. People were all around us. Fortunately none had come into the trees and discovered us. We were at a crossroads and villagers were busy with their everyday duties. A couple of times someone would step off the trail into the edge and satisfy their bodily functions, yet no one seemed to look up. I glanced around. Everyone was awake by now. Gradually the sun began to sink to the west, and traffic slowed down around us. We waited until it was almost dark before we slid down and stretched our cramped muscles and joints. Silver and Dusty were having a whispered discussion off to one side. Finally, we all huddled. A plan had been formed. We had inadvertently stopped at the road we were supposed to get on in order to reach our objective. We were only about an hour away. Once we reached the prisoners - or rather, abductees - and freed them, we were to take a road that went due east toward the coast, an estimated two hours travel on foot. There we would rendezvous with Vietnam Special Forces that would extract us. We were not to speak in English until were clear of the captors. Ok, I had lots of questions, but now wasn't the time.

We walked silently along the road. We had opened the bags we had jumped with, and were now wearing black pajama tops and coolie hats. We concealed our weapons. We occasionally would meet someone, but never offered greetings. Soon we approached a village. On the south edge stood a 2-story building, a nondescript mixture of colors and quite ageless to the look. We watched for several minutes, then slipped back into the brush.

Silver said, "We need to rethink this. We are too early. We can take one of the cars and be at a pickup point in a few minutes instead of an hour or more. Boots, can you disable two of the vehicles? I nodded yes. "Pick a good one for us" He replied, "Good. Make the entrance with us, then when we are in control, go take care of it. For now, everyone rest. I am going to take a closer look."

An hour later he returned. "They are there," he said. "Both upstairs. Two guards downstairs, one upstairs on the north balcony. One left a few minutes ago headed for the village. It is 0100 now. We go in in exactly one hour. You three, two through the front door, one through the back. I am going to get the guy on the balcony. Everyone get your heads in the right place. There is no margin for mistakes."

Well, this was not what I had in mind when I had gone to the recruiters' office in Tucson months ago. Nope, I had a different picture in mind. I though to myself.

One hour later we very quietly surrounded

the old building. Silver disappeared toward the back. On cue, we entered the building. The two guards were asleep at each end of the room. They never had a chance to get fully awake, Dusty and his partner took care of that. A sound from upstairs, then quiet. Weapons came up, then Silver appeared with a thumbs up. I turned and went out the door. One of the vehicles was '49 or '50 Ford pickup with a tarped-over frame on the back. I was familiar with this. My father had one. I walked around it and opened the door. *Thanks, people.* The key was in the ignition, and I fired it up. It had a half tank of gas. I went to the other two automobiles and punctured a tire on each side, one on the rear and one on the front, with my machete. As I was puncturing the last tire I became aware of a pair of boots coming around the front of the vehicle. Something was said in Vietnamese. I just came straight up from a kneeling position with the machete point up. It entered his body just at the belt and went up through the bottom of the rib cage. He never made a sound. A river of blood ran down my hands and arms. I wiped it off on his clothing, jumped in the little pick-up truck and backed it around to the front door. As the three others emerged with a Vietnamese lady and her child, they picked them up and put them in the back. Silver and the other guys piled in behind them. Dusty climbed in the passenger seat said, "Go! Go! Go! That way!"

We drove through the village, and at the edge of town turned onto a better road. I drove as fast as I could without attracting too much attention. Soon I could see the glisten of water in the small amount of moonlight we had. We approached a small dock area. Dusty jumped out, and I saw his flashlight come on one, two, three times. Almost immediately it was answered; one, two, a short wait and three.

"Let's go," he said. Everyone got out and went running down the dock. We piled into a junk, a small motor started, and shortly we were at sea. Two or three hours or so later, I kinda lost count, we rounded the small point and entered the bay at Da Nang. We were safe!

Later that afternoon Silver and I caught a flight out of Da Nang and were back at the Continental for dinner. Our conversation turned to the past 24 hours.

"Silver," I asked, "Have you done this type of thing before?"

He laughed. "Not quite the same thing, but the same type of work. Listen. What we have got here is, we are doing the work that Vietnam Special Forces are supposed to be doing. President Deim pulled a bunch of regular troops out of his army and made Special Forces of them. But what he did not do was train them. They would have gone in last night with guns blazing." He paused. "If they had even been able to get there, everybody would have been killed, including the lady and the child. We did the whole thing without even firing a shot. By the way, I saw the guy laying there by the car, Boots. I assume you did that? What happened?"

I related the incident. He nodded. "You acted totally on instinct. That is what you have to do to survive in war. Good job!"

For the next few days, we did little except for my training. We made some trips to the Embassy and did a little sightseeing around the city. Saigon was truly a beautiful, although strange, city, with many different customs that a country boy such as myself found different. One day as I was walking down the sidewalk in a somewhat residential part of the city, I observed a young Vietnamese lady walking toward me. She was a typical Vietnamese girl, beautiful with long dark hair, and dressed in the traditional high collared tight fitting top that reached down to her ankles, but it was split up the sides to her waist, revealing white silky loose fitting pants that also came to the ankle. The dress was called an Au Dias. Traditionally, it was worn by both men and women, but in later years only by women. As she approached me at about 20 yards, she suddenly stepped off the sidewalk onto the grass. She quickly lowered her trousers, squatted and urinated, then pulled her pants back up, stepped back on the sidewalk and continued past me. I was never so surprised in my life. Holy Cow! If a man or woman had done that where I was from they would have been in jail immediately!

CHAPTER 3

Our next assignment came a few days later. He was a member of President Deim's staff. It had been discovered that he was selling info for opium. The Vietnamese seemed to have a weakness for the drug. I knew almost nothing about drugs at the time. Later on I came to believe that centuries of subjugation by various conquering cultures caused deep depression in much of the people, and that opium helped to soothe it. He was a relatively easy mark, having a habit of long walks in wooded gardens near his home. I stood lookout as Silver stepped from behind a tree and sliced the man's throat. By now I thought little of it. It was just a part of the job.

As Silver rejoined me I remarked, "That was quick and easy," and his only reply was a quick look at me, and silence. My thoughts were what did that mean.

A few days later I retired to my room early. I had gotten a book on Vietnamese history and culture and was busy devouring it when I overheard loud voices coming from Silver's room next door. Then it was quiet again. I resumed my reading and finished a section that Marco Polo had written about the people of Vietnam. At one point they had devolved to a point where they had eaten their own history books. My head spun at the very thought of that. Then there came a knock at my door that I knew to be Silver.

"Come in."

He entered. "After tonight I want you to keep your door locked, and keep some kind of weapon handy. Ok?"

"Ok," I answered. "What's wrong?"

"Nothing yet. But we have been noticed. And we have just been handed the most dangerous assignment yet. We need to do several days of planning and training for you. Get a good night's sleep. We are up early tomorrow, and busy for a few days."

We caught a taxi early next morning and had our breakfast at the Embassy. After breakfast we went to a room near the back of the Embassy. A man unlocked the room saying, "Be sure and lock the door when you are finished." Silver nodded. The room was a clutter of different things, several of them being weapons of different sorts. But there were clothes, hats, shoes - lots of things.

We walked around for a few minutes, looking at all the stuff. Silver picked up a piece of piano wire about 30 inches long with two pieces of about 3/4 inch wooden dowels affixed to the ends.

"Do you know what this is?"

"Maybe," I said. "Not really sure."

"It is a garrote," Silver remarked. "Think you could learn to use it?"

I grinned. "Maybe, 'cause I bet you're gonna teach me, ain'tcha?"

All I ever saw was the quick half grin that was his usual! We picked up several items and we placed them in a beat-up old overnight case.

Silver said, "Meet you down in the garden where we train."

"Ok."

I walked downstairs and out into the garden and found me a seat on the low wall where I lit up a Chesterfield King. I had smoked about half when Silver appeared with a basket of fruit and vegetables. I looked at him.

"Silver, I'm not real hungry right now."

Again the quick grin. He sat the fruits and cabbage and melons on the wall, all at shoulder height. He took the garrote out of his pocket.

"Pay attention."

He put one of the dowels in each hand stretching the wire tight. He reached his left hand on the right side of the cabbage, looping the wire around to the front and left, and he jerked the wire tight, neatly slicing the cabbage into two pieces.

"You get the idea. You try it."

For the next few minutes I waged death and destruction on the helpless fruits and vegetables. When I finished with slicing the watermelon in half Silver was particularly elated.

"But just remember, you must get it below the chin, really important for it to work, and you must be very quick. They can't get their fingers under it."

Later, it sobered me somewhat to think I could take someone's life so nonchalantly.

We got back to the hotel. We caught a cab to a really fancy place Silver knew of. It turned out to be a restaurant on a rooftop. Lots of people. British people, French people, Chinese people, and high class Vietnamese people. The food was excellent, about three or four different courses. On the way back to the hotel Silver was even more silent than normal. As we approached my door, he nodded for me to follow him. We entered his room and walked out on the terrace. I always enjoyed the sights of Saigon below me. The smells, the sounds, all so foreign, yet intriguing We sat down and lit up cigarettes.

"Boots," he said, "I felt like I owed you this tonight. This thing we gotta do is probably way over your head. We have got to plan this very carefully. There are dozens of things that can go wrong, and we are not going to have much of a support group. I didn't want to take this job the other evening. There doesn't seem to be any one else to do it at the moment. Tomorrow we are going to scout it out. Maybe for a couple of days. We don't want to be seen doing it. If anyone suspects anything we will be dead. Tomorrow dress really casual. Wear a coolie hat and oriental shirt. Don't talk to anyone, don't look directly at anyone. No eye contact at all. Now get some sleep, early day tomorrow."

Right. You tell someone something like that, then tell them to go to sleep. I went down to the hotel bar and got a cold bottle of Coke and took it back upstairs. I picked up my book of Vietnam history, figuring this should put me to sleep. After several chapters and several Chesterfield Kings and the bottle of Coke, I turned out the lights and lay down. The overhead fan turned lazily above my bed. The sounds of the city played outside my window, like a strange radio station. *God, I should have got hit by a truck, that day on the way to the recruiting station!* Not only the feeling of loneliness in a very foreign place, but the uncertainty of where my life was heading created a deep sense of anxiety. Soon the myriad of possibilities faded into dreams of little Vietnamese men and women pursuing me through the streets of Saigon.

The next morning as the sun came up over one of the many branches of the Saigon River, we watched the first rays settle on the little houseboats parked along the shore. As we came around the bend, a large, dark, slightly foreboding building came into view. It was made of every kind of cast-off piece of material one could ever imagine. It set about 4 feet off the water and extended perhaps 50 feet into the river. A long ramp of sorts led from the long point of land that jutted into the river. Several boats were tied up around it, and it had a walk-around deck that totally surrounded the building. There did not appear to be anyone stirring. Our driver kept his speed steady, and we continued on up the river without steering any closer.

Silver muttered, "Sure would like to see inside."

We continued up about a quarter mile, pulled into an secluded spot, and got   an hour or maybe more. Slowly the river came alive. We pulled out and continued upriver for a mile or so and found a new spot to park. We sat for some time, dozing in the heat. Finally around   mid-afternoon we headed slowly down the river. When we got in sight of the building the driver cut his engine until we were almost drifting. We lay under some bamboo matting, with our glasses trained on the building which now had mats pulled back from the doors and windows to let the breezes flow through in the tropical heat.

Several men sat around on boxes and mats. We could see several weapons stashed back in the shadows. A girl or two came into view, both bare-breasted, and Vietnamese music drifted across the water. I saw one guy lift a bottle to his mouth and drink long from it. Another came to the edge of the deck, opened his pants and urinated into the river. He looked long at us - we lowered ourselves even more. As we came closer, the boatman cut the motor. He got up and hovered over the little outboard cursing loudly in Vietnamese. We drifted slowly by, our eyes drinking in every detail. As we came abreast the little motor fired and, with a cloud of smoke, we were on our way again. After we rounded the bend we stood up, letting the air cool us from lying under the mats in the heat.

Silver looked concerned, we must see the place at night.

The next evening again found us in a boat on the river, a different boat this time. We repeated the exercise from the day before, we quickly passed the building at about 11 at night and again at about 3 in the morning. At three in the morning activities had subsided and there only seemed to be about four men on the boat and three or four girls. It appeared to be a possible brothel. There was definitely a lot of drinking going on, and the girls were always in various stages of undress. No one seemed to be carrying long weapons, although we could see two or three of them standing among the boxes. The next evening was the same, except a large boat was pulled alongside the dock, and bundles and boxes were being loaded from the boat.

When we got back Silver took a deep breath. "We have to do this thing tomorrow night. I want to see what was in those boxes if I can, but we can't wait any longer."

He pulled an envelope from a suitcase and held out a picture. . In it a young Vietnamese man looked back at me. He looked (to be) about 20, a small slender man.

"Boots, this is your target. He must be taken out, but you gotta be careful. We know very little about him, except that he is an NVA Officer - Army of North Vietnam. He is way smaller than you but as you know, that doesn't mean much. You must stay focused, don't give him any chance. Here is the plan!"

The plan was we were going in by boat again. The boat would let us off just above the bend in the river. Silver, being smaller, would go in first. We were disguising ourselves as Coolies - a little brown shoe polish on hands and faces, big hats and native clothing. It scared me to death every time we did this. I was way too big for a Vietnamese man. I was to wait three minutes then follow him. There was a central room in the building that seemed to be an office. We figured this was where I would find my man. I only had three minutes from the time I went in until our ride home would be alongside. We would be taken to another location to spend the rest of the night, hopefully, *if* everything worked out right. I spent the rest of the day alone.

I read for a while, and I smoked way too many of the Chesterfields. I thought about home, and going hunting with my dad. I remembered as a kid, I would catch a rabbit sitting, and I would circle it, getting closer when I would get behind it. I would jump it, and catch it with my hands. I smiled. My dad would say, "You're better than a hound dog." Yeah, Dad, I had better be tonight. I practiced all the things Silver had taught me, and I tried to remember all the things my Grandfather Chris had taught me about stealth when you are hunting. Grandpa's father was a

Confederate soldier who went all the way through the War, indeed he was in some of the worst battles. He saw thousands of men die; some were his friends and neighbors. Won't people ever change? War never solves anything. And here I am. It really isn't a real war, but they say we are protecting innocent people. Anyway, I can't have any of this in my head tonight.

I dozed for a few hours. A knock on my door awoke me, it was dark. Silver said, "Let's get ready". We went down the back stairs with our gear to a waiting car. On the way we slipped the loose fitting pants over our clothes and the blousy shirts over ours and colored our faces slightly. We arrived at our boat, boarded, and rode silently up the seemingly empty river. We made a quick pass up the river past the building and then back. It seemed quieter tonight than last night. We landed just around the bend. We walked the short distance to a clump of trees about thirty feet from the building. Silver tapped my wrist. I raised my arm; he held his wrist next to mine. Our watches had been set previously. He looked at me and held up three fingers. I nodded. He tapped my eyebrow, and made a move that I knew meant 'eyes open'. Again I nodded. He turned and walked to the ramp, then stooping slightly and with little short steps he was up the ramp and into the building. I watched my watch. It looked as if the second hand wasn't even moving. *"Get a hold of yourself!"* I said to myself. As the second hand approached the third minute I took a couple of deep breaths and stepped out. I walked as much like Silver had as I could, making myself as short as I could. As I stepped onto the deck, I turned left and went around the building. A hallway went towards the center of it. Looking down I saw an AK-47 sitting by some boxes. I picked it up and laid it behind some bags and continued on. Just as I was getting close to the office a girl stepped out and said something to someone inside. I melted into the dark, and stepped out in another hall to the deck. I saw another AK. I picked it up also, and with a rope that was used to tie boats alongside the docks, I lowered it into the water. I stepped back into the hallway. I looked at my watch. A minute and a half had gone by. Damn. I reached the doorway. I recognized the man sitting at the desk from the picture. I reached into my waistband and pulled out the garrote. Moving swiftly ,but as quietly as possible, I approached his back.

He obviously heard me. He started to speak, but as he did I circled his head with the wire, pulling it tight around his throat, jerked it, and lifted him out of his chair. Blood spurted, then the sound of air bubbling as it rushed out of his lungs. He stiffened and then started to go limp. I heard a noise behind me, and I turned as a man rushed at me. I literally threw the body on him, knocking him down and backwards. I twisted his knife from his hand and shoved it into him up between his ribs on his left side, covering his mouth as I did. He didn't move.

I looked at my watch. I had fifteen seconds. I went to the deck as a small boat was still drifting into place. I hoped this was the right one. I grabbed a rope and swung over the side. As I touched the boat, hands pulled me down. The boat motor revved and we were pulling away, a girl screamed. Voices started yelling. Just as we rounded the corner, an AK began its pop-pop-pop sound, but we were gone. About a hundred yards away I heard a bang, then a huge explosion lit up the night sky! I looked at Silver.

"Silver, what in Hell did you do"?

Grin! "I didn't do anything, I wasn't even

there. I guess when you have an arms dump you should be careful where you leave things laying around"

"Uh huh!" I laughed "I guess you expect me to believe you had nothing to do with that?"

Then came the grin again. We went a short distance downriver and pulled to shore. We got into another car that was waiting for us. We didn't go back to the hotel that night. We stripped our clothes off and dumped them, washed our faces and hands in a fountain outside in the plaza, and spent the night at a club with lots of people around. We had been concerned for a while that we had been noticed in our comings and goings so we wanted to be seen that night in a much different environment.

I slept most of that day, waking just before sundown. I lay for awhile in thought of the previous evening's activities. It was hard to comprehend that someone with my background could do some of the things I had done in the past weeks. It just wasn't me, or at least I didn't think it was me. Did my uncle, as soldier in WWII, do these type of actions? How did he deal with it? My great grandfather, during the Civil War, a much bloodier war than anything I could imagine. How did he handle it? But this is my job, how do learn to take pride in it? A Chesterfield King seemed to soothe my troubled brain. I walked to the window and looked out across the busy streets. The normal evening activities were being enjoyed, dinners being eaten, people sitting in the fading light, conversing, and having a drink with friends. One would never suspect the other darker things brewing in the background.

I slipped on my boots and jeans and shirt, and went down stairs and out onto the sidewalk. I found a vacant table and ordered some food and a Coke and lit up another Chesterfield as I waited. A middle-aged couple sat down at the table next to me, nodding at me as they did so, while voicing a quiet "Good evening." After placing their order, the lady turned to me and asked, "Do you speak English?"

I couldn't help smiling. I don't believe I had ever been asked that in my entire life. "Yes," I smiled. "I do, or at least some version of it".

She laughed. "I do believe I detect a bit of a southern accent! Are you in the military?"

My brain froze for a moment. How do I answer her? "No ma'am. I am here on a college research program studying the Vietnamese culture."

"Oh, what school are you with?"

My brain spun for an answer. "University of Texas in Austin!" I spurted out.

"Well, that's very nice. My husband and I are from Santa Barbara, California. We are here for our twenty-fifth wedding anniversary. We are taking a tour of the South Pacific and some stops here in Southeast Asia. We saw the movie *South Pacific* and decided we just had to do it."

"Well, I hope you enjoy yourselves. But my advice is to keep to the populated areas and don't get off on the side streets. Saigon is a beautiful city but it can be dangerous, especially at night."

We chatted for a while longer while finishing our dinners and smoking a cigarette. I thanked them for our conversation, rose from my seat, and bid them a good evening.

I walked down Tu Do Street aways, wandering in and out of the shops, looking at all the beautiful clothing and artistic objects for sale. I think this is where I first smelled incense burning. It imprinted itself firmly into my memories, for whenever I think of my time in the old city I can still smell the fragrances floating in the warm tropical air. I made my way back to the hotel, and as I approached the curb a young Vietnamese boy of about ten approached me.

"Number One G.I., let Number Ten shoeshine boy shine his shoes!"

I laughed, "Ok, but I am not a G.I."

He looked me up and down saying, "You look like G.I."

He gave a good shoeshine job and chatted while doing it, mostly about America, and how some day he was going to go there. I mostly just listened and chuckled at him, but it was a bit unnerving that he made me as being military. I paid him and thanked him. I went back to the hotel and found Silver at the bar. I sat down and ordered a Coke, and related the story about shoeshine boy.

He thought for a minute and then said, "We probably shouldn't stay here much longer."

I told him about the conversation at dinner. He laughed saying "That was really good. We can keep that as a cover story. I'll be your professor!"

"Ok, Professor, but I had better get good grades!"

The next morning I couldn't find Silver, so I decided on one more trip to the market. It was alive with smells and people. I purchased several things, eating them as I walked around. I was almost out of the market and headed back to the hotel when I was bumped and felt a hand in my back pocket. I never carried anything in my back pockets, but kept everything buttoned in my shirt pockets. I snapped my hand down and caught the hand, came up with it, twisted it and chopped across the elbow. I heard it crack, and a yell of pain. For the first time I saw who the culprit was - a boy of about 15 or 16. I thought *Oh shit!* But true to my training I had reacted. I released him and he turned and left me. I looked around me. There were some really angry faces looking at me. Time to leave. No panic, just be calm and leave. I turned to find my way partially blocked by two young men on bicycles. I looked down at the old lady at my feet. I pulled some kind of a bill out of my shirt pocket and handed to her and I pointed at the boy and said, "For him." She nodded. I turned and walked straight at the two men on bicycles, looking them right in the eye. As I approached they separated and rode away in two different directions. I kept walking.

As I walked, I would glance in windows for reflections behind me, but no one was following. I breathed a sigh of relief as I stepped into the cool lobby of the Continental. I walked into the bar and ordered a Coke. As I sat drinking it, I collected myself. Silver slid onto the barstool beside me, saying, "You look like you just saw a ghost!" I told him my story.

"Yeah," he said, "That's why I said you have to be careful. One night I took a taxi to Tan Son Nhut, with a taxi driver that I had used before. He turned down an alley where a couple of other guys were waiting. I had the fight of my life, and then I had to drive that little ol' piece of shit Renault back myself. We have a price on our head, you know!"

We decided that night we had to leave the beautiful hotel. Boy, I hated that. I sure loved that place. The next morning we went to the embassy. Dan was there, and we told him about our feelings about the situation. He agreed, and then he told us we only had one more job in Saigon anyway. We took a taxi back to the hotel where we decided we would take one more stroll down Tu Do Street before heading out. We had talked many times about how much we enjoyed the city and the neighborhood around it. As we walked along conversing about the things we saw in the shops we went by, we heard a commotion in the street behind us.

We turned, and Silver said, "Let's step inside this doorway. That is Diem coming. Try not to make eye contact with any of his guard. We will stay inside here until he passes."

I nodded ok. As the procession of white motorcycles passed and another car of dignitaries went by, a white convertible came into view. In it was a man dressed in a white suit, his hair combed back, lounging in the back seat with his arm draped across the seat beside him. This was Ngo Den Diem, President of South Vietnam. To the right down the street the convoy screeched to a halt. An old man pulling a large two-wheeled cart had not made it across the street in time.

For delaying the royal procession he got a rifle butt in his back and was dragged into the alley and dumped by two of the uniformed guards. With hardly a halt the procession moved on. As Diem passed by, I couldn't help thinking, *You smug bastard*! Silver evidently read my thoughts. He looked at me, "Don't even think about it".

That pretty much ended our afternoon jaunt. We started back to the Continental. After a few minutes I looked at Silver, "And we are doing all this shit for that Asshole?"

Again he said, "You absolutely must keep that out of your head. You will see many things that don't make any sense, but for your own state of mind you can't think about it. Not now, not ever. It will weaken you, and it will get you killed".

We picked up our meager possessions and went to an address out near Tan Son Nuht. The house was walled; you had to go up to the second floor to see over the walls. We were told to keep ourselves out of sight, not to advertise our presence here. It would only be for a few days and then a car would come and pick us up in darkness and drop us off the same way as before. The next day our ride arrived. It took us to Tan Son Nhut where we went to the motor pool and picked up a jeep. Silver drove us over to the International airport terminal and we parked right out front.

After about 15 minutes a strong, hearty voice yelled, "Hey Silver! How you doin'?"

I looked to see a tall, slender but very well-built, athletic black man throwing his bag into the back of the jeep, then vaulting into the back seat. Silver answered, "Doin' fine. Meet Boots. He's my sidekick. Boots, this is Powder. He is gonna be our roommate for a few days."

I nodded and said, "Howdy, Powder."

Deep down I was dying to know how he got a name like that. He didn't look like any kind of powder that I had ever seen. He glanced down at my shiny Noconas, and remarked, "Yeah, I can see that."

He wrinkled his eyebrows and smiled, saying, "You better keep them locked up, I like them."

I grinned, "Uh huh, keep your fingers off my boots."

We rode back to the big hanger, dropped

off the jeep, and went into one of the offices that I had first been in when I initially hit the country. We went into a conference room, and as we entered, I noticed Dan sitting with three other men that I recognized from past encounters.   They   greeted   us   and pleasantries were exchanged. We then sat down around the table.

One   of   the   other   men   spoke   first, "Gentlemen, we have a very difficult task. We will first explain our dilemma, then we will ask for your suggestions. Firstly, this is the place." He held up a picture of a beautiful house. "It is across the river from Ben Hoa, and downriver a mile or so. Secondly, this is the man, or one of them." He held up a picture of a man probably in his early fifties, wearing   a   military   uniform.   I   thought, Vietnamese Navy, but I wasn't sure. I was unsure of his rank as well.

"The   house   is   being   used   to   store munitions   being   brought   in   from   North Vietnam and Cambodia, mostly by boat. We don't know yet how it is making the first part of the journey. This man is the person in charge. As you can see he is Vietnamese military and sits in pretty high circles. At the moment I prefer you not know his name. This is very sensitive. He must be removed and the munitions destroyed before they can be sent into the field on the wrong side. Powder, because of your specialty, this is why you were brought aboard. Questions?"

Silver stood saying, "I would like to see some maps and more pictures of the place if possible. Do you know how many guards? Also, is there any chance we could get close and check it out?"

The second man stood and said, "Yes, to most of it. As for getting close, probably no closer than a half mile maybe. Here, go through this and see how far it gets you. Then we will see how much more we can give you."

He tossed a yellow manila envelope on the table. The next two or three hours were spent pouring over the documents and pictures. I was particularly interested in the maps. At one point I leaned over and commented to Silver that I thought scouting it out from the river seemed like a good idea. He nodded approval. We went back to the house that evening and I proceeded to get acquainted with Powder. I discovered he had grown up in the area of Texas where Stephen Austin had settled in the 1830's. His ancestors had been slaves picking East Texas cotton. His parents insisted he get an education, and he had been able to study at a good college. He had joined the army during the Korean War. He liked the military and had stayed in for some time. He had studied architecture in school, and had trained in explosives in the military. When he left the military the CIA had recruited him and he had been doing work for them ever since. All this I learned from listening to the conversation between him and Silver. As the night wore on we discussed how we were to enter the building that was our objective. It seemed that this particular operation had to show no signs of US involvement whatsoever. With that thought I drifted off into a restless sleep.

The next morning our driver picked us up about 0700. We went up to Ben Hoa, then we were taken down to the river where we boarded a decrepit, smelly, old junk. We slowly headed down river. We had donned our coolie outfits and stretched ourselves out like a bunch of lazy day workers. As we drifted by the objective, Silver snapped some pictures of the dock below, and more of the house. I spied a tall skinny building about three or four stories tall about 300 yards downstream, close to the river. It looked abandoned. I whispered for Silver as we drifted by to take a picture of it, and he did so. We went about a mile downstream, then turned around and putted back up to where we had originally started, taking more pictures on the way. On the way by the second time, we saw a couple of men with weapons sitting in the shade of a tree at the rear of the building.

We got back to Ben Hoa and had our driver take us to the Embassy in Saigon where we left the film from Silver's camera. We spent the remainder of the day as if we were tourists, having good food and sightseeing, with an occasional bar stop for Silver and Powder to quench their thirsts. I never enjoyed the bars. I had never liked alcohol in any form, so for me it served only as a people-watching opportunity. Later, about 1900 hours, we returned to the Embassy and picked up the pictures we had left. We returned to the house and spent the evening pouring over the pictures and discussing different strategies. At one point I told Silver that I thought a person with a rifle could cover most of the building and the courtyard from the tall skinny building.

His asked me "Can you do it?"

I answered "Yeah, I think so."

Powder asked, "Silver, do you think you can make it up that tree at the back and get onto the second floor?"

Silver scrutinized the pictures again. "Yeah," he said.

"Then a plan is hatched," said Powder.

"All I have to do is get onto that lower floor." Silver continued "I will take a rope, and if there is any downstairs access, I will help you up the wall."

The next day we went over more details. That evening, our driver arrived at about 2200. Silver said, "Come on, Boots, we are going to check out your perch."

It was only a 30 minute drive to the building. The driver dropped us off with instructions to come back in 30 minutes. The building was deserted. It was also not secured. We made our way up two flights of stairs to the third floor. The side facing the building that was our objective had several big windows, a very good view for what we needed. About 20 feet back from the window was a big storage cabinet about chest high, and there were some bags on the floor. I picked up several, and threw them on the cabinet.

"That will make a great rest for the rifle, and this far back from the window will muffle the noise from the shots and mask the muzzle flash."

"Good idea." Silver grinned. "You *are* getting a handle on this game!"

I laughed. "Kinda like deer hunting in the desert, you don't want to give away your position right away."

We watched the building for a few minutes. Soon a boat pulled up to the dock, and several men got out and started carrying boxes up to the big door. One went to the right of the door, and as he did he reached up and did something, and the other man pushed the door open.

"Did you see that?"

"Yeah." Silver answered.

We could see five guards. One on the

second floor near the front, and one on the center back, near where Silver was about to enter. Two were on the ground near the back gate, and another seemed to be wandering all around the building. We made our way back downstairs and stood in the shadows until our car pulled up. We got in quickly and returned to our house.

The next evening was lit only by a quarter moon, an ideal evening for an operation such as the one before us. There were plenty of dark shadows, with hints of highlights here and there for navigation. My driver dropped me off at about 0100. I cradled the new Sako 'Finnbear' sniper rifle in my arms and climbed the stairs to the third floor vantage point. Dim lights from the target building enabled me to see the locations of the guards. I set up some bags and padding on the big storage cabinet. As I laid the rifle in place, pointing it at the windows, I moved into position behind it. I looked around. I was about 20 feet from the windows. The room would contain some of the sound and the muzzle flash shouldn't be visible from very far away. I leaned over. The stool I had found put me in perfect position.

I put my eye to the scope. The building below fairly jumped up at me. Wow, I'd never used a scope that good! I quickly found all five of the guards. Now it was just a waiting game. About 35 minutes later, I saw a small boat slide up along side the low dock. Two men dressed in the familiar black pajama-like clothes and coolie hats climbed out and started throwing bundles of something up on the dock. I watched for a moment, then fixed the crosshairs on one of them as he looked up. There was Silver's familiar face. I grinned. For security reasons I had not been told how they would approach the building. But there they were, and it was show time.

I watched through the scope as they each picked up a big bundle and started toward the gate. As they approached, the guards stood up, their weapons hanging loosely in their arms. Silver and Powder walked right up to the two men and then in unison threw their bundles on top of the guards. They went down on top of them and when they stood up again, the guards didn't move. Silver turned and looked straight at me, then went to the tree near the left side of the gate and disappeared for several moments. Powder disappeared near the right side of the gate where the hidden latch was located. I saw movement in the edge of my scope. I raised it and saw the guard up top had spotted the action below and was just pointing his weapon over the side. I dropped the crosshairs to his head and squeezed, and he disappeared off the deck.

Seconds later, I saw Silver come up over the rail on the deck. I moved my scope around and located the other two guards. They were still where they had been. I waited. I glanced back where Powder had been, the gate was slightly ajar. He was nowhere to be seen. Silver had disappeared into the back entrance of the second floor. I scanned the roof again. No one had moved. Five minutes passed, then the guy at the front closest to me abruptly spun around, bringing his weapon up as he did. I brought the crosshairs to the center of his spine, up high, and squeezed the trigger. He dropped. I looked for the remaining guard, but he wasn't there. I scanned the deck two, three times. Still, no guard. Then he appeared from behind the upper level near the rear, crouched down, moving slow, watching something I couldn't see. *To hell with it.* I brought the crosshairs to his upper body and squeezed again. He dropped to his knees, dropping his weapon and rolled over on the floor and was motionless. I waited another five minutes, then ten.

Finally, Silver appeared at the door. He looked up at me and held up his hand. He disappeared back into the building, and a few minutes later he and Powder emerged from the back gate, ran down to the dock, and jumped into the boat. They backed out and disappeared into the darkness.

About a minute after they disappeared, the whole building just seemed to swell up, and then it exploded straight up into the sky and fell back on itself. Then it all lit up into another explosion which illuminated the surrounding area. I pulled out the small bottle that I had been given and, by the aid of a small flashlight, I poured its contents into the muzzle. Then I poured some into the breach and into the scope. The acid bubbled, I was quite reluctant to destroy such a marvelous piece of equipment, but that was orders. I had never liked taking orders, and now found myself in a position where I must. I swiftly made my way downstairs and waited a few seconds as my car pulled up. I jumped in and was safely back at our house in a half hour, where my partners were waiting.

Silver lifted his beer and Powder as well. I opened a Coke, and we toasted to our success.

I asked Silver if the man was home. Silver laughed, "He still IS!"

I laughed, "Don't know about that, he may be in Ben Hoa. You guys didn't have a view of the place going up like I did!"

It was laughter all around. For a few minutes, I didn't feel anything about the men that had died tonight. Was I supposed to?

CHAPTER 4

The next morning we loaded up our gear. Our driver picked us up about 0800, and we drove out to Tan Son Nhut. As we entered the conference room, the three or four men sitting there stood up and clapped their hands loudly. Congratulations were voiced all around. Finally we were all seated.

Dan talked about our immediate successes, including last night, with all the accolades as to the appreciation from the South Vietnamese government. After having a late breakfast at the mess hall in the big hanger, we went to a small room in the back corner. Dan and another guy I had seen before came with us. As we sat down Dan began to speak.

"Silver, you and Boots are going to get to do something really interesting really soon. I think you really will enjoy the assignment, but first I have something else I need you to do for me. The Air Force is going to set up a ground mobile radar site outside of Pleiku. I want you guys to go along with them. There are some people you are going to meet that will be important to you. Go over this afternoon and draw weapons and ammo and field equip. You will be gone for a short while, so supply yourselves well. Everything is set up, you are expected. Powder, my friend, we have another plane ticket for you. You are on a plane tomorrow. I don't know any more than that."

Turning to us Dan said, "You guys, drop him off at the airport tomorrow, then go to Ben Hoa. Here are your instructions. We have temp barracks for you for tonight. Again thanks, and well done!"

As the others walked out, I turned to Dan, "You have a moment, Sir?"

"Sure, what's on your mind?"

"I would like to know what is in my records that made you choose me for this duty? It is nothing I have ever trained for."

He smiled, "Boots, you might be surprised. Everything in your life pointed you to this time. Your schooling, your aptitude, your family history. We looked at several young men before we chose you. Be proud. We consider you a very valuable asset to our organization. Now get outta here."

"Right, Sir. Thanks. I think."

Powder and Silver tossed back a few that evening. After we had dinner I watched "South Pacific" in the hanger theater. The next morning we had breakfast, then drove Powder to the airport. We had a few minutes before his plane boarded, so we sat in the jeep and made small talk. As we were talking, a little old lady came walking up, looking at us with a puzzled expression.

"Are you boys in the army?"

You would have to be able to see us to understand her curiosity. We were in basic civilian clothes, but we hadn't shaved in a few days - which wasn't a big difference in my look, but for the others it was. Silver and I were wearing 'Aussie-Go-To-Hell' hats with one side snapped up. We were armed to the teeth, in an olive-drab colored jeep. Obviously a little different.

Without even blinking an eye, Silver turned to her and calmly replied, "No, ma'am. We are security for a big plantation west of here."

She looked at him and said, "Well, thank you very much," and turned and went on her way. We all laughed and shook hands all around. Powder vanished into the busy airport, and Silver and I drove away to Ben Hoa. I wondered, as we drove, what was up for us now? So much had happened to me in so little time. Little did I know that in a few short weeks life was going to change for me in many ways. Life, as I had always known it, seemed to be as distant as it would be if I had changed planets.

At Ben Hoa we caught a hop with Air America and we flew into a place called Pleiku, in the central highlands of Vietnam. Air America delivered us intact; that was somewhat of a feat seeing as how the runway for the airport reminded me of one of dad's newly disked fields back home. It could scarcely be called a runway. My thought on landing was *God, I hope he makes it out of here!* It was a different world than Saigon, with all its bustle and activity. A jeep picked us up and took us to the tiny building that served as the headquarters for whatever military presence it was that served here. An Air Force Captain was behind a table covered with maps and various other things I didn't recognize. Silver identified us to him.

He looked at us quizzically. "Just what are you fellows supposed to be doing for us?" he asked.

"Whatever we might be useful for, Sir," Silver answered. "Actually, the powers that be thought I might be of some assistance to you. I have spent some time up here before. I understand the Degar some, and I have a general understanding of the countryside. Boots here is my partner; we are a team of sorts."

I looked at Silver. *Well, that was news to me,* I thought. I wonder what else this guy has up his sleeve that I don't know yet.

We talked for awhile with the Captain. We found out that we had a couple of days before we were to begin the operations. We were told of a spot to stow our gear and sleep that night.

We headed out, and as we came around the truck parked out front, two girls dressed in long ankle length loin cloths with bare breasts walked by me. One was carrying a young child. They were both beautiful. I just about lost my footing.

"What-tha....!" I stammered.

Silver said quietly, "You will get used to it.

They most all dress that way up here."

"You could have at least have warned me"

He laughed. "What? And miss out on that look on your face? Never!"

We found our tent and stashed our gear. Then we found the mess hall of sorts, and fed ourselves. Silver said he was going to catch some sleep, but I had to check out my new surroundings. He admonished me to keep my wits about me and my eyes open, that I was in unfriendly territory. I would never have guessed. I slung the little Carbine on my shoulder and walked out.

Up ahead on a small rise were a few rows of thatched-roof buildings built on stilts. I headed up that way. I walked up the street, trying not to look like a fat American tourist on vacation for the first time. The men and children seemed happy and friendly, with ready smiles. The women were slightly detached, a bit aloof. I walked a circle through the village, coming back down toward a small motor pool where uniformed military were loading some big boxes on a flatbed six-by.

As I walked by one of the boxes slipped.

The young airman reached to steady it. It was too big, and he was losing it. I jumped over and grabbed the bottom, and between the two of us we kept it from falling until another airman was able to help us secure it. We knocked the dirt off our clothes and the young redheaded stranger said, "Hi, I'm Mike Manus. Thanks a lot. I think that sucker would have squashed me, had you had not been there."

"You're welcome." I said. "They call me Boots."

"Boots, huh? What are you doing up here in this out of the world place? I'm from Butte, Montana, and I thought that was pretty remote!"

Yeah, this is a pretty remote place. My new found friend Mike advised me that he was off duty now and was gonna buy me a beer. I followed him to tent with a few snacks and beer. I thanked him but told him no on the beer, but that I would take a Coke. He nodded his approval. We sat for a couple of hours and I listened to Mike talk about his life and his plans, thinking it was good to hear someone with plans he could voice. I couldn't really do that. I had absolutely no idea where

I was going, or even what the next bus stop was going to offer. Many times I thought to myself, *This can't be happening to me, someone up the line has made a terrible mistake. You have confused me with someone else.* I always half expected someone to show up and say "Hey, come with me. Your CO has been looking for you. Where have you been....." but they never did.

About that time Mike jarred me out of my cloud. "What about you, Boots? What are you doing here?"

"Following my partner around"

"You Army? How come no uniform?"

"You really don't want to know." I laughed. "Hey, this has been great, I really enjoyed the visit, but I gotta get back to my tent. Maybe later."

I left so I wouldn't have to answer anymore questions that I didn't know how to answer. The next day as we prepared to move into the jungle, Silver advised me about a lot of stuff I needed to know. Most of which I don't remember now, probably because I didn't listen closely at the time. We spent a lot of time talking about the Degar. I had a million questions that swelled when I found out that he had lived in a village with them in the recent past. I was surprised to find out that they were the original people of Vietnam, an ancient people. The lowland people were immigrants from China over the last 5000 years even up to the last two or three hundred years ago. They didn't speak the Vietnamese language; their names didn't even have the same sounds as the lowlanders. They had different customs, different religions, different lifestyles. Very pagan in their beliefs, with a touch of spiritualism, they somehow reminded me of our Native Americans of the 19th century, yet different. They were hated by the Vietnamese, and they hated the Vietnamese back. That knowledge would come to haunt me in months to come.

That evening we went to the camp's watering hole. It was rather empty as we arrived, being a bit early. We grabbed our drinks and went outside and sat on the fender of a jeep someone had parked there. I lit up a Chesterfield King, and we watched the sun go down over a dished-top mountain to the southwest of us. Another day in Southeast Asia.

"Silver," I asked, "What do you tell people when they ask you what you do?"

He grinned one of those Silver grins, "Doesn't much matter," he said. "Different things to different people. It's none of their business anyway. Depends on what I want them to believe. If I am going to work with them, it might be one thing. If it's someone in a bar," he laughed, "it might be anything!"

"How long have you been in this line of work?" I asked.

He laughed again. "Since you were in junior high I reckon."

As usual, an answer that really wasn't much of an answer! The guy was an enigma, just no figuring him out.

As we stood there in the early darkness, the figure of a Montagnard man materialized out of the shadows. He stood slightly in front of Silver. He barely glanced at me and spoke in a language that I had never heard before. He talked for a few moments, Silver answered in the same language a few times, and then he was gone.

Montagnard man

I asked, "What was that all about?"

Silver answered, "He wanted to know if I was coming back to his village. It is up near Dak To. He said the NVA are moving supplies down the Ho Chi Mihn Trail, and he said they are trying to get his village to help, even by threat. He is the son of one the tribal elders. I need to talk to the boss about this tomorrow."

The next day two Sikorsky helicopters came in and picked up all the equipment and the next thing we knew we were setting down on a mountaintop a few miles to the west of where we started. Silver and I and a group of twenty or thirty Yard soldiers set up a parameter a short distance from the Air Force equipment. They got busy putting the site together, and by dark we were pretty much secure and they were operational.

Vietnam was never particularly a pleasant place; there was always some thing rather unnerving about it. But it did have its beautiful places, and the Central Highlands held most of these. I sat on the side of the hill looking off to the east, wondering what was out there; there were no lights, no signs of human habitation, nothing to grasp as a spot of security. A couple of Yard soldiers sat down below me, one to the left and one to the right. Occasionally one would look my way totally expressionless. I smiled to myself. Not a friendly face in sight.

It was late evening before my relief came. I had set my bedroll up before going on watch, so I wouldn't have to do it in darkness. It was a comfortable place, off to side of the camp near a large tree. I kicked off my shoes, bringing them inside the mosquito netting that I had put up and tucked under my bed. I slid in and was soon in dreamland, living in a world of girls in skirts and blouses and riding in '57 Chevys and '55 Fords, hanging out at the burger shop. I think I was just starting to feel the loneliness after the all the madness I had experienced.

The first ray of sunlight broke through the canopy of trees and hit me full in the face, bringing my slumbers to an end. As I raised myself up on one elbow and squinted into the sun, something an almost iridescent pink moved about 10 feet out from my feet. I strained to focus on the object, and lifted myself a bit higher. When I did, the object raised itself a foot or so off the ground, and I could see the hood behind its head fan out. *Oh shit, a King Cobra!* I froze. I could never get out of the bedding and all that mosquito netting and get far enough away in time to avoid its strike. I lay there for what seem like an eternity. Then one of the Yard soldiers appeared. He said several words to me, none of which I understood. He walked to the edge of the clearing and cut a small sapling of bamboo with his machete. He then shook it at the snake. It turned its attention to him and started to move away from me. As soon as I saw it go I came out of the bedding, taking the netting with me as I went, much to the amusement of the other Yard men that had appeared. My heart didn't slow down for hours!

I sheepishly picked up my gear and squared it away, put my shoes on, and went to the mess tent. Although I had never drank coffee before, and still don't, I had a cup that morning. I wasn't much in the mood for eating. I toyed with a helping of SOS and toast and jelly. Silver came in and sat down.

"You look like you have seen your own ghost," he laughed. "I heard what happened. We're not in Kansas anymore! I'm not from Kansas, but this morning, Texas would look really good! Well, anyway, we are going for a walk today. About ten or twelve miles to the east."

We packed our gear, and set out about 30 minutes later. We followed a road that really was mostly just a trail. I began to lose my shock from the morning and settled into our journey. I was amazed at the trees and the vegetation. It was like reading one of the travel magazines my Grandpa used to sell subscriptions to, only I was there, not only experiencing the landscape but the smells and the feel of the place too.

It was almost dark when we walked into a clearing containing several buildings that had the earmarks of western architecture. I guessed they were French, and shortly I was proven right when a lovely lady in a white dress stepped out of the house onto a porch and addressed Silver in French.

"Bon jour, Monsieur Silver."

"Bon jour, Alaine."

She and Silver turned and entered the house. I motioned our small company to rest and sit down on the porch. It was comforting, something like going to Grampa's house and sitting on the porch except I was surrounded by 12 or so Yard men and countless miles of jungle. In a short while, a man who appeared to be Vietnamese came out and took the men to a building that I supposed to be something like a bunkhouse. He returned shortly, just as two women appeared bearing containers of food. He motioned them towards the bunkhouse, then turned to me, and in very good English with just a touch of a British accent said, "Sir, would you please come inside with me."

I followed him into a dining room. Silver was already seated at a nice table with comfortable chairs. The lady he addressed as Alaine was seated across from him. At the head of the table sat a man in his early 60's. He looked like someone I would have met at home at a Farm Bureau meeting. His hands were strong and calloused. He was slightly balding, but the hair he had stood tall and wavy. A striking man, to say the least.

As I entered, both he and Alaine turned and smiled and greeted me in English and asked me to make myself comfortable. Would I like coffee or tea? I chose tea. I had never liked coffee.

Silver said, "This is my partner, Boots. He is new to this part of the world."

Again, both issued words of welcome. My tea arrived.

We spent the evening discussing the hostilities in the country. Vietnam, it seems, had always been at war with someone, from the Nguyen rulers to the French Colonization and the Viet Minh that eventually overthrew them to the Viet Cong uprising of recent time. In between there had been times of peace, but Silver and I both thought this is going to turn into a long and bloody war.

Silver had evidently known our hosts for some time, so after a bit of food, I excused myself and went and sit on the porch. I lit up a Chesterfield King, blew the first puff of smoke into the night air, and settled back against a post and looked up into the night sky. Millions of stars stared relentlessly back at me. I could have been at home on my own front porch. I thought of my friends at home, wondering what they might be doing. Hanging at the hamburger joint? Or the local gas station, bragging about how fast our cars would go. I suddenly felt a pang that could have been homesickness. Then, after a thought, realized I now seemed to be a stranger not only to them, but to myself.

Silver appeared beside me. "What ya doing?"

"Oh, I took a trip back home. I just got back."

"Everyone OK?"

"They didn't recognize me."

He frowned slightly, a bit puzzled at my answer. He motioned for me to follow him to a small building. Inside were a couple of tables and a couple of bunks at the end.

"G'night." he said.

"Yep." was my response.

CHAPTER 5

Next morning at breakfast I found out the reason for our being here. The CIA wanted to put an intelligence base up here close to the border to monitor the "Trail". We were here to scout it out and make recommendations. The Ho Chi Minh Trail had been used by the Viet Minh in the French Indo China War to transport men and goods for the fight against the French. It came out of North Vietnam into Laos, and down through Cambodia to almost to Siagon, with several branches connecting it to South Vietnam.

Silver instructed me to take a couple of the Yard men and set up a perimeter and to send a couple out for lookouts, and to set up a signal procedure in case we were to get unwanted guests. I picked a spot for myself on a rise where I could see the buildings and the men and some of the terrain to the northwest. I found my spot just outside the elephant compound, an enclosure of about an acre. I sat just outside looking over a small hill, not totally exposed, and made myself comfortable leaning against the fence. After a couple of hours, I noticed one of the elephants staring at me. I had heard them and smelled them the night before. My experience with these massive creatures was nil. I had only seen them in the Zoo and once when a circus had come to town. Watching them was fascinating. I decided that they must all be females, but thought the one watching me was a male. After further inspection, I realized she was just larger than the others. She was definitely Boss Lady over the others. When she had something to say, they listened.

I kept a close eye on the jungle out in front of me and the road that appeared for a few hundred feet about a mile away. Deep down I hoped nothing showed up. I was tired of all this war stuff. During the next few days my mind went back to home a lot. One thing was interesting though, that big elephant. Every day as I appeared to work my shift, she got a bit closer. She watched me a lot. I had always had an affinity for animals, except for dad's cows - they gave me cause to become especially proficient at profanity. That wasn't allowed in my home, but out in the pasture, after four or five tries at getting them to the barn, the air would fairly smoke from the words coming out of my mouth!

I watched the elephant every day. Finally, on the fourth day about mid day, I was intent on the scene in front of me when I heard a slight whisper of breath behind me. I knew it must be her. I remained very quite and didn't turn to look at her. Finally, after what seemed like several minutes had gone by, she reached her trunk out and touched my shoulder. She moved her trunk slowly around my shoulder and close to my face. I could smell her breath. Then, just as quickly, she was gone. I turned to look and she was several yards away. I wondered that something so big could be so silent in her movements. She never again came to see me or appeared to be particularly interested in me again.

We spent another couple of days at the plantation, then a chopper appeared. We said our goodbyes, and Silver and I were away again on another adventure.

We flew back to Pleiku, and in a day or so, caught another Air America flight to Da Nang. We checked into the MAAG-V offices there, and were given some quarters. It was a small base, but near a town that offered a small bit of entertainment. But I found I missed the quiet and solitude of the plantation.

One day, as we drove to another location - I am not sure where - we were driving along a tree lined road. The terrain was fairly flat. We rounded a bend and there, sitting in this grassy field was this Buddha. A fat, round Buddha, sitting cross-legged quite flat. The top of Buddha's head must have been 40 or 50 feet from the ground. It was truly amazing. My first thought was, *I'm not in Texas anymore, for sure.* I will never forget the sight of that huge Buddha sitting there.

We traveled a bit for a while. Silver seemed to have lots of connections. I knew he had been in the military for a long time, but there seemed to be something different about him. I wondered what his real job was, and what was I doing with him? Why me? I tried to broach the subject several times, but he would just change the subject and the conversation would just go another way, but I always wondered.

We wound up back at Da Nang and I found myself being something of a crew chief on a helicopter, transporting ARVN out to the jungle and dropping them off. It was fairly easy duty, until the VC started shooting at us. Didn't like that at all! I wanted to be on the ground where I could at least duck.

About the third or fourth trip out, we were coming into a hot Landing Zone. I could see the cleared spot about a hundred feet below. We were coming in fast. I turned and looked at the soldiers and raised my arm for them to stand up. They did. As I motioned for them to get ready, about that time the pilot side-slipped abruptly, and I stepped out backward.

The last time I looked we were about a hundred feet up, Everything got really slow, I said goodbye to everyone I knew, maybe even a few I might want to meet sometime, then suddenly I hit. I didn't die, but I couldn't breathe and I couldn't move. And the chopper was coming right down on top of me! Then it stopped.

Two young Vietnamese soldiers picked me up and threw me back in on the floor of the bird. I was just starting to get a few gasps of breath. I still couldn't move. All the way back to Da Nang I thought, *is this the way my life is going to end, paralyzed?* I was scared to death.

We landed, and stretcher crew loaded me up and took me to the field hospital. After a while a Captain, a doctor, came in.

"Young man, are you aware you have no

dog tags or other identification?"

"Yes, Sir. You can just call me Boots. Get a hold of Silver over at MAAGV headquarters, Sir."

"I will do just that. But first, we can't find anything broken, but you have probably just about pulled everything apart. We are going to give you a couple of days, and if you don't get better we will ship you out."

Well, I didn't get better. So they sent me to Clark AFB in the Philippines. After a week all my feeling came back   and I went back to Da Nang. Silver picked me up at the airport.

"Sure glad to see you," he grinned. "I didn't want to have to train another partner. You were working out pretty good."

"Ok," I laughed, "But you don't have to get overcome with emotion! But, believe it or not, it is good to be back. This place looks real good compared to what I thought my end was gonna be."

He nodded, "Understand. By the way, we had a hell of a time explaining to the Captain why you were running around in Vietnam with no identification. Finally someone at MAAG came down, pulled rank on him and told him to shut the hell up. But if you run into him again, just tell him you can't comment on it."

The next few days were spent getting back in shape. I'm telling you, hospital food will kill you, and you add military hospital food to that and it's worse. I ran everyday, I did push-ups and sit-ups and pull-ups until I would just fall into the bunk at night and die. Then I had the opportunity of doing combat training with a bunch of ARVN boots. That was a real kick. I was 6 to 7 inches taller than the tallest one of them and 40 pounds heavier; it was probably what saved my life in later days.

A few days later we walked into MAAG-V in Da Nang where we met with a couple of guys I did not know, but evidently Silver did. The conversation went something like this:

"Silver, you had mentioned some friends in a village up near Dak To that were being pressured by VC."

"Yep, thought you had forgotten."

"No, we had not forgotten. Actually, most of the Yard villages up along the Cambodian and Laos borders with Vietnam are coming under that same kind of pressure. Intel has it that the NVA is planning on turning the Ho Chi Minh trail into a munitions supply line. They are obviously going to make this a big affair."

Silver and I looked at each other.

"So, what's next?" Silver asked?

"Well, we are going to send some people up to the villages, teach them how to defend themselves, arm them if necessary, and try to back them up. We don't want to lose these people. They hate the Vietnamese anyway, we can use that. We have people in Laos that are doing the same thing, as well as watching infiltration. You and Boots have been selected to go up there. Come back tomorrow at 0800 for your briefing. And think about what you want to take with you. You can advise us of that tomorrow."

We went back to our quarters. Neither of us spoke for sometime. I, mostly, did not know what to voice. I had not the slightest inkling of what was ahead. After a trip to the mess hall, we ate and smoked - or at least I smoked, as I enjoyed my Chesterfields.

Silver spoke. "Boots, you might want to think about quitting those for a while."

"Huh?"

"Well, we are going to live a very different lifestyle for a while, starting real soon. There are several reasons why, I won't dump them all on you right now. By the way, do you feel like you are back in pretty good shape now, after your injury?"

"Yeah, good as new."

"That's good. You are gonna need all your strength and endurance, coming up real soon."

Well, at least I had something to mentally chew on now.

"One last thing. Write a letter home. Tell whoever is there that your job is going to take you out where it is going to hard to get and send letters. Tell them to not worry if they don't hear from you very often. Mail it. Then write another letter and make it you last will and say any goodbyes that you wish. We will keep it here at headquarters in your records. Understand?"

Now I did have something to chew on! I nodded.

Later, after taps, I sat down to write. The

first letter was pretty simple. Small talk, things I could talk about, questions of life at home, the usual. I advised them of my coming situation, and signed off. I addressed an envelope, inserted the letter and sealed it, and tossed it on the table near me.

Then I took out another piece of paper and stared at it for several minutes. My thoughts became jumbled. How do you write something like this? Oh Yeah, *Hey Folks, when you receive this I am already gonna be dead. Sorry to let you know like this, but I have been busy killing people, and shit like that. Your loving son. Oh yeah, my name has been changed as well as everything else, I am called Boots now.*

I sat for almost an hour. Finally, I wrote:

'Dear Folks, don't know how much of this gonna make sense, but I have been given a job to do. I think it is a very important job, and will benefit some people that need a lot of help. I can't go into a lot of detail, but it is kinda dangerous and there is always a chance it won't all work out as planned. I don't have a lot of valuables to disperse if that becomes necessary, so that is not going to be a problem. I have always been taught to

be honest and forthright in my dealings, and to treat everyone as I would like to be treated. I intend to follow those rules that I have been taught. I am appreciative of my care and upbringing, and I pledge to never bring dishonor to my name. I have always been taught to work hard at what I do. I still do that, and I take great pride in what I have accomplished so far in this life. If fortune chooses to cut me short in days, then so be it. I am where I chose to be. If you are reading this, then I have already left this world, and an adventure in the next has begun. All my respect and love, I ask only that you remember me as I was in your favorite memory.'

I folded the letter and slipped into an envelope and sealed it. I turned it over and wrote *To be opened only upon my death* and signed it.

Next morning I met Silver for breakfast. I had dropped the first one at the mail facility, I handed him the second.

"That was the hardest thing I have done since I arrived in this God damned place. By the way, where is yours?"

"Oh it's around." Another half smile. "It's so

old, it's written on a scroll of parchment."

We walked the short distance to MAAG. After waiting about 15 minutes for the rest of the Brass to arrive, we were finally seated. Silver handed a few sheets of paper to one of the operatives that had been present the day before. The only remark was, "Holy Shit, you gonna set up a trading post?"

Silver rather icily replied, "Naw, I just wanna feel important!"

Next day, we caught a chopper out to Dak To. It wasn't much, just some Special Forces. The village we were headed for was in the 3 corners of Vietnam, Laos, and Cambodia. We were closer to Laos than anywhere else. We caught an Air America ride for the last part of the journey. There was no place to land near the village. The pilot made a couple of low passes over the hamlet, wagging his wings, then headed straight north a couple of miles off to a hilltop that had been de-brushed to some degree.

As he made his approach I looked at Silver, "He's not gonna try to land there, is he?"

He answered, "I hope he does a little more than try!"

"Oh shit."

The top of the hill wasn't as long as a football field. It wasn't level either, and it had bushes throughout.

"Crap, I can see why you made me write that letter!"

The pilot made his approach into the wind. From below the crest of the hill, powering up just enough to top the ridge, he hit the edge of the clearing and immediately set it down. By the time we had stopped we were at the other side of the clearing.

"Silver, you know I don't drink, but I think I may start."

The pilot turned in his seat and handed a small flask back to me. We all laughed.

"Just kidding, I knew you could do it all the time," I lied.

We unloaded our gear, which was considerable. I knew we couldn't carry all of it, but within a few minutes we were surrounded by about 10 or 12 Yard men clad only in long breechclouts. They were all smiling and gathered around Silver and me and were shaking hands and talking all at once. Silver did more smiling than I had seen him do in all the time I had known him. It looked very much like he had just arrived home to his family. An older man spoke and our gear was immediately scooped up and, except for personals and weapons, we had nothing to carry. The small plane sputtered to life, and the pilot wheeled it around until it was headed back the way he came in. My heart was in my mouth. It looked suicidal. He revved the engine until I was worried it would fly apart. He released the brakes. It jumped forward, bouncing out toward the canyon in front of it. I wanted to hide my eyes. At the end of the field it disappeared. *Oh, God.* Seconds went by feeling like minutes. Then there he was, climbing back out of the canyon. He circled back over wagging his wings, as if to say, "told you so," and turned and vanished into a misty cloud. The men all cheered loudly, then picked up our gear and disappeared into the jungle. We followed.

It was a short walk. We soon came into a clearing which housed several smaller hooches, smaller than the houses I had seen in Pleiku. They, too, were on stilts, but not quite as high as the bigger ones I had seen. As we entered, women and children of all ages gathered around us. The children without exception were all naked. At some age, probably about twelve I was guessing, they seemed to start wearing the long ankle length breechclouts. The women were all bare breasted. They were all different. Some were very beautiful, all seemed quite healthy, and all very, very curious.

Now you have to remember, I grew up in the area of the Bible Belt where you would have probably placed the Buckle if there was one. And to be standing with half-naked young ladies, reaching out and touching my head and face, and generally being very unabashed in their efforts, was quite discomforting to me.

We were taken to two small huts next to the edge of the jungle about fifty feet from each other. We dropped our gear, and then escorted to a larger building. The largest building in the small hamlet, I guessed it to be something of a community center for lack of a better description. Everyone sat or squatted oriental style. The older man from earlier stood and spoke for a few minutes, making references to Silver. Then another man who was a bit younger, probably forty or so, addressed Silver.

Silver stood and spoke. I listened spellbound to the conversation. He made gestures that I did not understand. Then he looked at me, and motioned me to stand. He said something that ended in "Boots", and everyone looked at me and smiled. I smiled back and nodded, and said. "Thank you."

By this time it was getting dark, and the women started to bring in baskets and pots of food. Awesome smells filled the air. Then someone carried a couple of spits inside, and my face must have paled visibly, because Silver looked up and said, "Relax, they are monkeys."

On the spits they looked like small children.

"They are delicious," Silver said.

"You should have warned me."

"Probably. I can't think of everything. By the way, eat everything you are offered. You don't want to offend anyone."

"Damn it, Silver!"

"It won't kill you. Oh, yeah, and keep it down too."

As we were served, I found most to my

liking. The monkey was good - I thought it to be something like squirrel. And the python was exceptional. There were different vegetables I didn't recognize, most everything was quite spicy. Then something was handed me. It was white, with a bit of brown where it had been roasting. I looked at Silver.

"Go ahead. You will be surprised."

He took one cracked it open and dipped into some kinda sauce and bit into it and said, "Do it."

I duplicated his moves, then took a deep breath and bit into something that felt something like Shrimp, but without the fishy taste. But it was quite good. I finished it with gusto.

"Now, what was it?"

"They are giant grubs. They are a delicacy."

My first thought was *OH MY*! But then I remembered crawfish back home, and suddenly they didn't seem so bad. After dinner everyone seem to melt away to their respective abodes. We did the same. We walked by my quarters first.

"Silver?"

"Yeah?"

"Is there anything else you should warn me about?"

"Probably."

He turned and walked away into the night. I climbed the couple of steps up to my lair and flipped on my flashlight. Lo and behold, my bedroll had been laid out and all my stuff had been stashed neatly against the wall! I scratched my head, uncertain of whether I liked the idea of someone messing with my stuff. But the events of the day quickly erased whatever thoughts I might have had, and sleep claimed me.

I awoke in basically the same position I had fallen asleep in. I rolled over on my back, stretched, and reached for a Chesterfield King. Oops, I forgot. I had left them in my personal gear in a locker in Da Nang. That was gonna take getting used to being without. My thoughts were suddenly interrupted with the sight of a young girl stepping onto the platform of my hut. In one hand she carried a bowl of something hot, and a pitcher of water. She motioned me to hold out my hands. I did, and she poured the water over my hands then took a cloth from her belt and dried them, then she handed me the bowl of food. She looked directly into my eyes and smiled brightly, and was gone. I sat for a moment overcome with the girl. Her beauty, the unexpected moment. I sighed, puzzled a bit. Then, taking a spoon out of my mess kit, set to the food she had brought, which turned out to be delicious.

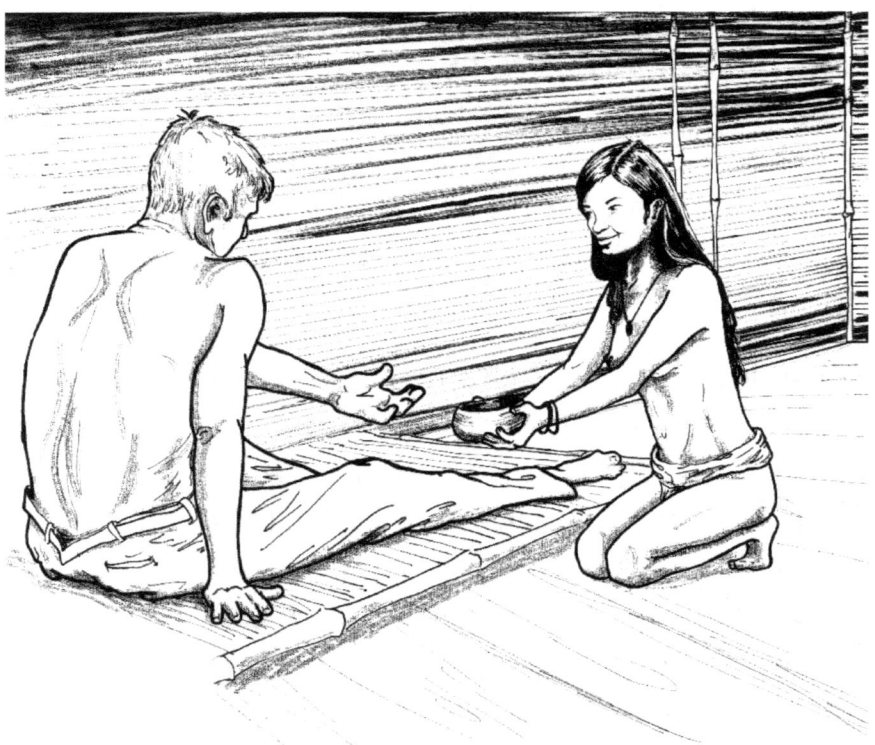

When I was done I cleaned the bowl thoroughly and set the bowl on the edge of my platform. I dressed myself and sat down on the edge of my deck, so to speak, and watched the village come to life. I re-laced the new boots that had become a part of our new uniforms, or *non-uniforms.* The boots had no manufacturing marks on them, no company names, no country of origin and neither did any part of our clothing, even to our underwear. Our shirts and trousers resembled common clothes that someone would wear if he worked in a hardware store. They were of a grayish-green color, the shirts long-sleeved, the pants a slack of some sort. They didn't particularly look American made. They were held up with a narrow black leather belt. The boots were of a brogan type, slightly taller, but not as tall as jump boots. We wore Aussie *'Go-To-Hell'* hats with the brim snapped up on one side. I carried a Colt .45 automatic in a web belt and canvas holster on my left side, I also had a M-2 Carbine and a Filipino Headhunters knife about 28 inches long sheathed in a water buffalo hide scabbard. I had a bag that I slung over my shoulder that carried other items and a couple of extra clips for both weapons. Silver was dressed similarly.

When I arrived at the center of the village

Silver was in conversation with some of the men. I listened without interruption. In a few minutes he stopped talking and said to me, "Good morning."

"Morning." I answered.

"We are going on a hunting trip today. You ready?"

"Yep."

Off we went. I had no idea what a hunting trip with a bunch of Montagnards would be like. I had hunted all my life, but this would be something new. The jungle was beautiful here in many ways. I had enjoyed all the jungle movies in my youth, Tarzan, Jungle Jim, and Sheena. Now it was my jungle adventure.

The men hunted with crossbows, they were extremely accurate. Within a short time we returned with several monkeys, some kind of a rodent looking creature, but bigger, and a small deer of sorts. I simply went as an observer. Watching these men hunt was one of the most awesome experiences of my life. I was to enjoy it many times and participate in it. We enjoyed the communal meals with the people. After a few days I felt a sense of family. When you got to down to basics, and overlooked the style of dressing and the level of technology and all of the more notable differences, there was the obvious. The daily living, the acquiring of food, the preparation and distribution, the raising of the children, with all the care that requires. I watched the daily activities. A wife getting angry with her husband, and vise versa. Two neighbors in a disagreement. It wasn't a lot different than what I grew up with, it just looked a little different. That thought gave birth to another thought. If we could just live in small communities we would probably be able to work out our differences more amiably. than when we become states of countries, because then we become subject to politicians and rulers that complicate our live immeasurably.

My second evening I sat alone in my small quarters, thinking of what the fates had given me. I thought of myself growing up on a farm, born of simple Christian people. People who were patriotic, religious, and innocent of most of the activities of the world. Unless these things were thrust upon them, such as war. My people didn't travel. Up until the time I left for boot camp, I knew of no one in my family for generations that had ever ventured more than couple of hundred miles from where they were born except for my uncle who had been in Europe in WWII. My innocence was being chiseled away at a rapid rate. I think that evening I was a little afraid of who I might become. As sleep crawled into my mind, the sounds of the jungle faded away, and the village was quiet.

I awoke with a start, sensing that I was not alone in the room. As my eyes focused the image of the young girl from the previous morning became clear. She was sitting cross-legged about two feet away from my bed, very quietly, just looking at me. I rose up.

"Good morning."

She smiled but said nothing. I noticed the pitcher and the bowl of food.

"Are you my waitress?"

Again, nothing. She lowered her eyes, then picked up the pitcher and motioned for my hands. I rolled to my side, holding out both hands. She poured the water over them then reached for her cloth and dried them. *God, her hands were so soft!* She looked at me intently as she did this, and I couldn't take my eyes off her. She then reached for the food and placed it in my hand, and turned to leave. As she did, I touched her wrist. She turned back. I said, very quietly looking into her eyes, "Thank you." Then again, "Thank you." She smiled ever so slightly, and was gone.

The next face to peer over my platform was that of Silver.

"Are you ready to go to work, or do you just want to stay here and let little native girls wait on you all day?" he asked with a typical Silver half smile.

"I'm ready. Wha'cha got in mind?"

"We are going down with some of the men to check out Mr. Ho's trail. Come on when you're dressed and ready!"

About fifteen minutes later, we were leaving the village. I remember heading out in a northwesterly direction, and down a well used trail. The lead man picked up a comfortable easy run; we continued this for about an hour. I was starting to breathe a bit heavy when we stopped for a breather. The Yard men were apparently used to this. Silver seemed quite comfortable. So after I rested a few minutes we continued, sometimes running, sometimes walking, for about the next two hours. Then Silver drifted back until he was along side of me.

"Keep your wits about you. We are getting close to the trail. Also watch for anything unusual on the trail, like booby traps." Silver whispered. We topped a rise, and there below us ran a road. Not a big road, mind you, but definitely a path well travelled. We settled into the hillside, in deep cover, and watched.

About an hour and a half later we saw two elephants with probably a half dozen men riding. coming down the trail about a quarter mile away. We watched for a while, then Silver said something to one of the men. He nodded. About seven or eight men slipped out of their hiding and disappeared down into the valley. As the two large animals got closer, I could see one of our men in a tree near the trail. As the elephants walked past, suddenly the men riding started falling. One of the men in the tree stepped off onto an elephant as it walked by. He kicked the dead rider off and sat down on the big animal's neck. He stopped the elephant and the other, in turn, stopped.

Silver stood up and said, "C'mon!"

We ran down to the trail. Eight dead men in black clothing lay in the road. The crossbows our men carried had been accurate and lethal. The men had made the elephant kneel and lay down. When we opened the bundles on their backs we found a load of munitions, AK-47's, ammo, some older Chinese rifles, bags of rice, and other valuable stores. Silver gave instructions to the men, and soon the bodies were all hidden away from the road. All but what stores we could carry were also hidden away from the trail.

By this time it was getting well into the afternoon. Everyone picked up what they could carry, and we started the long trip home. By the time it got dark, we were back to the good trail, but it was still not a safe place to travel at night. We set up a perimeter and a guard schedule, and after the labors of the day, I fell asleep quickly.

Just as it was coming dawn Silver nudged

me. We picked up our loads and started out. In a couple or so hours we arrived back at our village. Everyone was excited. I felt like I had been on a Shawnee hunting party with my g-g-g-g-great-grandfather Daniel.

After things kinda calmed down a bit, I walked over to Silver. "Hey, I'm getting kinda funky. Where can I take a bath?"

He laughed. "Follow those women with those jars. Take a towel and soap."

I went back to my hut, grabbed my toiletry bag and a towel, and headed out. About a hundred yards or so down the trail I came across a beautiful little stream. There were three pools and a couple of small waterfalls. Two women were filling some tall jars. We passed without greeting. I went downstream around the rock to a small pool with a five foot waterfall pouring into it. I looked around me. No one was around, so I removed my clothes and stepped into the water. It was cool but not cold. I stood under the waterfall, then stepped out and soaped down, and then went back and let the water run over me. It was delicious. My body was feeling the strain of the last two days. I stood there with my eyes closed, enjoying the sensation of the water. Then came the giggles. I opened my eyes. About thirty feet away stood two young women and three children, staring intently at me. It was the children giggling. My blood ran cold, and my first thought was to run and cover up. Then I caught myself. These people are not afraid of nudity; to react that way would not be good. So I casually turned away and picked up my safety razor and proceeded to shave. As soon as I had finished, I stepped out onto the rocks, toweled myself off, and redressed in clean clothes. A new man thusly was born. I picked up my stuff and nodded to my audience, smiled and said, "Good afternoon!" and walked back up the trail.

As I walked by Silver's hooch, he was sitting cross-legged in the doorway.

"Wow, shaved and everything. What are you trying to do, make that little girl fall in love with you?" he was laughing as he finished.

"Not really," I said. "I have never liked being dirty. By the way, how do I handle that situation? I can't find anything in the military manual about it. What am I supposed to do, pay her for being my maid? How do I react?"

"Just be nice to her. Don't offer anything

except kindness. No overtures of affection or anything like that. To give her a gift would mean you are trying to court her, and I wouldn't advise that."

"OK, did someone tell her to do it, or was it her idea?"

"Beats me, time will tell."

I turned away, then stopped. "Do you have one?"

Silver laughed, "Not yet."

I went to sleep that evening without eating. I slept straight through until morning. When I awoke my little maid was sitting beside me again.

"Good morning," I said.

Only a smile, then the hand washing ritual, then the food. When she handed me the bowl I held it steady in my hands before she released it. I looked at her lovely face.

"Thank you," I said, "Thank you."

And then like a kitten, she purred something soft that I didn't understand, and she was gone. I sat there for a moment, thinking about her. But all I could do is shake my head. Silver was right. One day at a time.

After I finished eating I joined Silver. We gathered the men together. We had about twenty five men that were to be soldiers. We picked a spot about a hundred or so yards from the village to set up a firing range. We lined the men up, set up some targets, and proceeded to teach them how to shoot their newly won weaponry. It wasn't a difficult job, and by mid afternoon most of them could hit their target at a hundred yards. We unloaded the weapons and returned to the village. Silver held a class on how to care for the arms, how to clean the weapons, etc. Then class was dismissed for the day. Later in the afternoon Silver and I sat down in the shade of a huge tree near the edge of the village.

"Well, Mr. Boots, what do ya think?"

"Well, Mr. Silver, about what in particular?"

"The raid on the Ho Chi Minh Trail. The Degar as soldiers. Staying here in the village. All of the above."

"Well," I said slowly, "I really like the village. What is to not like about being served breakfast in bed by a half naked young lady? As for the men as soldiers, I have a feeling that I am going to learn more from them than they are going to learn from me. They are naturals. They know the country, they fit this type of warfare. I'm glad they seem to be on our side. But, Silver, I am never going to like this killing thing. I can do it, but I don't like it"

Silver dropped his head. "No one expects you to like it. Just keep your head together about it, and remember you are no more guilty of this than that .45 on your hip. You are a tool, to be used to accomplish a task. When it's over you can go home and feel no guilt. You mustn't think about it like that."

"I try to keep it in that perspective, but it wasn't in my upbringing to do this. I try to be very mechanical, and just let training take over. It isn't easy!"

The next few days were spent in teaching our little legion of 25 to adopt a militaristic point of view. They tried very hard, but sometimes I wasn't sure if they were laughing at us or pissed at us. But all in all things progressed quite smoothly. One thing that bothered me was they just wanted to carry their weapons in their hands hanging straight-armed, or sling them over their shoulder. Finally, one afternoon I took ten of them and put them into one group, and ten into another. The remaining five or so I had stand out in the edge of a clearing and watch. The first ten I had Silver take aside and tell them how to hold their weapons at ready, barrel forward at waist height. The other ten we told nothing except that when the two groups came into each others view, to start firing. Of course we had unloaded weapons first and inspected them carefully. We told them to point their weapons and go *bang! bang!* very loudly. We then took them into the jungle in two different directions, and pointed for them to come out at the clearing. Sure enough, when they hit the edge of the clearing, the ones with arms at ready started aiming and going 'bang, bang' before the others could even get ready. The point was made, and from then on they were always at ready.

The men were diligent in every respect. I soon came to admire them, and grew to like them. Indeed, I liked all of the people. I had a familiarity with them, almost a sense of family, I bathed in the same river, washed my clothes like they did, ate their food, and slept in the same kind of bed they did. I felt like a Degar. Except I was a foot taller and 60 pounds heavier.

In a couple of days we made another trip to the trail. This time, we took more time getting there. We set up observation points on hilltops several miles apart until we could have a relay from us to the trail. The last one on the line could see movement on the trail ten miles upstream with a set of binoculars. He could use a mirror to signal the next one in line and so forth all the way back to the village. We also made food and ammunition stashes along the route. We used some of the younger boys, not yet old enough to use as soldiers, as the lookouts. We spent all day watching the trail, but no one showed. We spent a long night in the jungle. Then, about two hours after sunup, we saw approximately a dozen men coming down the trail about a mile up the road. Silver pointed to two of the men that were acting as Sergeants, and motioned them to us.

"Boots, take Duk and his men down to the trail and take cover on the other side. Wait for my signal, or gunfire, whichever is first."

We made our way down. Our men vanished like ghosts into the brush. The convoy of men came into view around the bend in the trail. These weren't Viet Cong, these were NVA. Probably advisors or trainers. We let them pass. Just then, all hell broke loose, the air was filled with the 'pop, pop, pop' of AK fire. I stood up and started picking off targets. Behind me Duk and his men did the same. The battle only lasted a few seconds, then it was over.

We cleaned up the mess, leaving no sign of the ambush. The bodies were disposed of far enough from the road that no one would find them. I looked at Silver, "You know what? We could do this for a year, and what have we accomplished but a few dead men? But we haven't slowed anyone down, this is bull shit!"

"Ok, what do you propose?"

"I don't know yet, but we gotta think of something."

"Well, we did find out we have a fighting force."

I grinned. "Yes, we did. But we did have them outnumbered, and we did have the element of surprise."

Silver frowned slightly, "And I hope we always do."

I thought about it for a moment then said, "Yeah, me too, I guess."

We went back to the village. One of Duk's soldiers, a young man named Malik, came and sat beside me. He looked over and smiled. With sign language he pointed to me and pretended to be me, then he raised his rifle and went 'bang', then made a motion of something in front of him falling. He repeated it three times. He then took the gun and pointed at himself, and then to me. I understood. He had watched me shoot. He wanted me to teach him to shoot straight. I smiled at him and nodded yes. We laughed and he patted my back excitedly.

I yelled at Silver, "This guy wants some shooting lessons!"

He nodded and gave a thumbs up sign.

The young man and I went to the ammo storage locker. I picked up a couple of clips for his AK, figuring he needed to shoot what he had, and we walked out to our firing range. We did prone first. I put him into position, and pointed at the target, and watched him. I held up my finger one time. Ok, he nodded. He aimed and fired. I motioned him to leave the rifle and follow me. We walked down range and I showed him where he hit to the right, and low. We walked back. This was hard to explain with out words. When I looked up, three more young soldiers had joined us.

I had him lay down near me. I laid down behind the rifle and took it properly in my hands, right hand circling the pistol grip, left cradling the front stock. I pointed at the top of the front sight. I picked up a piece of a twig, then held it with the top of the twig barely showing in the rear sight. I looked at him. By then all four young men were in a semi-circle around me, laying on the ground, very intent on what I was doing. I took a fairly good breath then let it almost out, held for a second, and said, "Bang!"

I looked around. They all nodded. They got it the first time. Then I took my finger and put it below the trigger guard, and pretended to shoot. I made a motion for them to watch my trigger finger, then I leaned down and took my breath, jerked the imaginary trigger, and acted like it was a bad shot off to the right. I frowned and said, "Shit."

Then I motioned for them to watch. I put my finger back and breathed, and then every so gently, I squeezed the imaginary trigger and said "Bang!" then smiled and said "Good."

They all smiled and said, "Good" almost in unison. Everyone laughed.

I then moved them a little more out of the way, of the weapons discharge, and the ejection of spent casings but allowed them to be close. I chambered a round and took my position. I took a breath, let it out, and squeezed off. Bull's-eye! I raised my eyes, looked around, smiled, and said "Good." They all laughed and said "Good" several times. Today we learned how to shoot and learned a new word. It was good!

I let everyone take turns. I corrected them when they made a mistake, and praised them when they did it right. We practiced kneeling and standing, and when we ran out of ammo we all walked back to the village together, brothers in arms. Getting back, Silver asked, "How did it go?"

I grinned. "It was great! Those guys are so sharp, they pick up on everything immediately, and then do it. They are really cool cats!"

He just looked at me like that ridiculous description.

Next morning, I awoke to find my guardian

angel beside my bed as usual. I raised myself up and said, "Good morning."

She smiled and said, "Good morning," not quite confidently, but clear enough in her small voice. I laughed. She seemed a bit startled. I restrained myself and said, very slowly, "How are you?" and pointed my finger at her, smiling. I then pointed at myself and said, "I am well." She put her finger in the middle of my chest and said, "Boots" and laughed a beautiful, melodious laugh. I joined her. I carefully pointed my finger at her, but didn't feel comfortable about touching her chest. I said, "You." She looked at me for a moment, as if unsure, then softly she said, "Sui." I smiled.

"Thank you, Sui." Only then did she wash my hands, and hand me my food. I smiled as she shyly turned away and was gone.

CHAPTER 6

We, meaning Silver and I, had just finished with a training class with the soldiers. We sat down in the shade. Even in the Central Highlands the heat was oppressive. I had grown up in the South in the time period before air conditioning in homes. At best we had fans, so I had dealt with heat all my life. But Vietnam was something else. I had an idea that had been brewing in my head for a while. So, as we sat down, I took this opportunity to put it to the boss.

"Silver, I have an idea."

"Ok."

"We know those troops and supply trains don't travel the whole trip non-stop. They must have staging areas set up at various points. Why don't we send out scouts to find these places, and when we find them, we hit them hard, and destroy their camps. That would cause them more grief than just an occasional ambush."

"You know, Boots, I think you are catching on to this type of warfare real quickly."

I laughed. "Well, my old Grandpa always said, 'If you are going to do something, learn to do it well.'"

So we went and talked to a couple of the village headmen. They were all for it. The next morning, four men headed out towards Laos. We continued our training. I kept working with my little sharpshooter group, and it wasn't long until they were deadly at 200 yards and fairly accurate even beyond that. I asked Silver if we could get a couple of long rifles down here. He said he would try. In those early days, we had a kinda difficult communication thing. About once a week, Air America would fly over in a small plane. If we had no need we would hoist a white flag. If we needed to talk we would hoist a red flag, and he would go to the strip and land. So about a week later we got a couple of WWII rifles with scopes - an Enfield 303, and a German Mauser. The first time to the range, I didn't know which was bigger - their eyes when they looked through the scopes, or their smiles the first time they fired the big rifles! They were happy soldiers. The same plane brought us in some explosives and some incendiary grenades. We were prepared to accelerate the warfare.

Our scouts had returned within a couple of days. There were actually three base camps on the trail that were within our reach without leaving the village unprotected for too long. So, within a few days we embarked on our first mission as an aggressor. The first strike was the farthest north into Laos. We reached it late in the day and scouted it 'til dark. About an hour before daylight we moved down to within a hundred yards of their camp. We hid ourselves and lay quietly, waiting for daylight. Silver had told me to button all my buttons and tie my pant legs and sleeves down, so nothing could get in my clothes. Just after dawn, I was grateful for that advice, as this nasty looking snake slid across my arm and went on its way. I didn't breathe or blink as it went by, and I couldn't stop shivering for several minutes after it was gone. Damn, I hate snakes.

Shortly after daylight, one lone soldier showed himself. He walked to the edge of the clearing and relieved himself. He turned back and went to the embers of a small fire and tossed a couple of sticks of wood on it. It was then we hit them. The Viet Cong and a couple of NVA fell immediately. A couple of women, probably villagers that had been pressed into service as mules, ran back up the trail and into the brush. We walked down to the camp. It wasn't very well staffed this day. One of my snipers, Malik, was busily looking over the bodies when I saw movement to my right. One of the VC sat up and was leveling his weapon at my man. I pulled my .45 and shot him twice. Malik turned when he heard the shot. He saw the dead VC and saw me standing with my pistol in my hand. He walked back to me, smiled, and shook my hand.

We figured probably a half dozen had escaped. We took all the arms and ammo that we couldn't use, and all supplies that we couldn't carry, and piled them up and set them on fire. We did as much damage to the site as we could, trying to make it as unusable as possible. We left, going down trail for several miles, then turning up a stream so as to cover our tracks. We didn't want to be followed home. We returned the next day, and when we reached the village a couple of the elders met us. They seemed worried. I took the guys to our storage hooch, and we stored everything away. Silver and the men talked for some time. When he returned, he told me that when we were away a squad of ARVN had come to the village. They were insinuating that the villagers were hiding VC, and had given them a bad time for a while. Finally, they had left, threatening to come back and burn the village if they found any VC.

The next day our little plane came over. This time it dropped a small parachute. It glided down, and one of the boys retrieved it. He brought to Silver. Silver opened the box and found a walkie-talkie. He keyed the mike and said 'Hello', or something to that effect, and the voice of our pilot crackled back through the speaker. The villagers reacted excitedly. Silver told him about our skirmish and about the ARVN visit, and told him we didn't need anything this trip. The pilot replied that he would pass along the info, and flew away.

There was a feast and a wine-drinking celebration that night in the village. Aware that I didn't drink, Silver warned me that the rice wine was lethal, even to drinkers. He said I should do it , but fake it as much as I could. I waited and watched as long as I could. The wine was in long tubes of bamboo, and they sipped it through long straws. They then refilled the amount they had sipped with water. I got me a cup of water and waited until few were watching. Then I pretended to sip, but actually took in very little. I then poured some water back into the tube. I must have gotten away with it; no one seemed to notice I wasn't doing it right. Or perhaps they were just too polite.

Later that evening, one of the young men came and took me by the hand and took me up to one of the "Kings". He said some stuff to me that I did not totally understand, then placed this metal bracelet on my arm and shook hands with me and smiled a lot. I smiled back.

Silver walked over to me and said, "Congratulations! You have just been made a member of the tribe. Probably because you saved that young man's life the other day."

"What," I asked, "does that mean? Am I supposed to act any different?"

"No," he said, "but you may find they treat you a little different. They obviously like you."

"Oh." I said, still a bit puzzled. Or was it that wine? It must have been the wine, because before too long I could hear my bed calling for me. I left the festivities, which were winding down, and slowly made my way to my hooch. I carefully climbed the notched log and slid onto my bed.

I lay there for sometime, trying to wrap my head around the events, and slowly drifted off. I awoke with a start, aware someone was in my room. I reached for my machete, then a soft voice said, "Boots."

I whispered, "Sui."

She lay down beside me, pressed her back up against me, and laid her head on my arm. My mind was a jumble of thoughts. *What am I supposed to do now? I am not ready for this, what to do?* Finally, I just lay down beside her and put my arm around her slender waist and snuggled my face into her hair. We both drifted away into dreamland together.

When I awoke she was gone. Was this a dream, created from that lethal alcoholic concoction that I drank the night before? I didn't know what to think. Then she was back with the water and the food, only this time she sat next to me on my bed. She was talking to me about something that I totally did not understand. She washed my hands, then taking a moist piece of cloth she cleaned my face. As I ate my bowl of food she continued to talk, occasionally touching me - my face, my mouth, my hair, my arm, or shoulder, my chest. I had decided I was going to treat this young girl like she was a King's daughter. I was going to be kind and caring and thoughtful and affectionate, but I was not going to even think about taking liberties.

After she had left to go about her daily duties, I joined Silver and the soldiers. I related the events of the previous evening.

He smiled. "You are doing ok, just let her lead the way."

"How old do you think she is?"

"She is a woman, doing a woman's thing. I would say mid-teens to late teens, maybe."

"Jeez, Silver. I was not looking for something like this, not even expecting it."

"I know you weren't. My way of looking at it is, she lives in a dangerous world. People are dying every day. You are presently living in that world as well. You two like each other. Be friends, learn from each other. Learn about each other's world. Be a comfort for each other, relax and enjoy life. You only get one."

He walked away. I sat and thought about his words. It was a little too much to wrap my head around.

I was brought back to reality by my little sharp shooter Malik. He sat down beside me and said, "Boots?"

"Yes?"

He pointed at a middle-aged woman and man sitting on the platform of their house about 30 yards distant. He first pointed at the couple again, then pointed at himself and pretended he had a baby in his arms cradling it. He repeated it.

"OH!" I said. "Your parents. Your mother, your father."

He nodded his head. We understood each other. That was great. He then made motion of rocking a baby again, and again pointed at the older couple. He said, "Sui," and smiled.

Oh My! This was Sui's brother, they were her parents! He got to his feet and took my hand and tugged on it, causing me to stand. He led me to where the older couple were sitting and took me up the little ladder and motioned for me to sit beside him. I did so. I remained quiet while he spoke to his father and mother. Then he turned and said, "Boots," as if he was presenting me or introducing me. The father spoke, and after a few minutes took my hand and shook it and held it and patted it and said something that was quite emotional to him. You could tell by the look in his eyes.

My young friend turned to me, and motioned for me to speak. I took a deep breath. I decided it wasn't what I would say that mattered, but the way I said it. So I said, "Thank you, my friend, for inviting me to meet your parents," acknowledging each of them in turn as I spoke. I smiled as I talked. I turned to the parents. "Thank you for inviting me into your home. I am a friend of your son's. He is a brave soldier, and you should be very proud of him. You have done well as parents." I ended with a smile. They had listened attentively to me, and smiled back at the end of my speech. Now the mother got up and returned with a cup of tea and a bowl of rice and some type of meat. I ate the food and drank the tea. Both were quite tasty. I ate in silence. When I had finished, I handed the cup and the bowl to the mother. I looked at both of them and said my warmest "Thank you!" My brain raced for what else to do. Then I thought, *My Chesterfields*! I reached in my shirt pocket. I only had a few, but I took out three, handed one to the father and one to the son, and put one between my lips. The men looked at it strangely. I motioned for them to do the same. They did. I took out my Zippo and fanned a flame and lit mine, taking a puff. Then the father, then the son each lit their cigarettes They took a puff and smiled. I did good! We finished our smokes, and the son and I stood. I bowed slightly, said thank you again, and shook the father's hand we, Malik and I left. I felt like it had all went well, and put my mind into the training programs for the rest of the afternoon.

We started putting out sentries in all directions so that we wouldn't get caught firing rifles by someone we didn't want to know, like VC sympathizers. We left before daybreak for the second camp on the Ho trail. It was farther south, near the edge of Cambodia. It took us all day and part of the next, traveling fast, and we made a camp some distance from the trail. We prepared some food and ate it, but no fires that night. We went into the trees to sleep, and early next morning we crept up to the trail. We could see a couple of water buffalo and an elephant, about a half dozen bicycles loaded with baggage, but no soldiers.

I turned to Silver. "This isn't right. Where could they be? These people should not be out here unprotected. Whaddaya think?"

"Ya, I agree." He called a couple of men over and talked to them. The men left, one heading up trail and the other heading down trail. We waited. Then about a mile up trail, a mirror flashed.

"That's where they are," Silver said. "Let's divide and conquer. Take your shooters up trail and set up for an ambush. We will go mess with their camp. Don't let 'em get us."

I motioned for my guys to come with me. We found a spot on a curve in the trail, about three quarters of the way to where the mirror flashed above the trail. I had the two guys with the big guns on the lower side, and the other four on the up side. I found a spot above the point so I could see both ways. About thirty minutes went by. Then down the trail came the sounds of small arms fire. Then, a couple of loud bangs. A few minutes later, here came a bunch of VC and a couple of NVA on bicycles. We let them get just to the curve in the trail. I picked one of the NVA, took aim, and squeezed off a shot. He went down, then the guys opened up all around me, and the VC started dropping, then the NVA. Three or four of the VC had jumped off the trail and we could see them in and out of the jungle. Then came the crack from the Mauser. I saw one of the VC fall forward. I turned to my left and saw my buddy, Malik, with his fist clenched and his arm raised, smiling broadly. I stood up and turned to face him, and did my very best hand salute. Then he smiled and shook my fist in the air. It had been a good 300 yard shot at a moving target. And just then, in the same moment, I realized, *Oh my God! You are just congratulating someone for killing another human being. Worse, and you taught him how to do it!*

I quickly shook the thoughts from my head, and we turned and hauled ass down the hill and down the trail to the camp. When we arrived, Silver's crew had mostly wrapped up everything. It was all burned and destroyed, the defenders killed or scattered into the jungle.

As the days and weeks went by we were

successful in slowing down Mr. Ho in his quest to overrun South Vietnam with troops and war supplies. Notice I said 'slow down'. There was no stopping what was to come, but we gave it our best.

One evening as we sat and discussed the events of the day Silver said, "Hey Boots, did you know that MAAG-V has set up listening posts all up and down the trail, watching for NVA troop movements?"

I grinned, "They could have just asked us, huh!"

"I wonder how much we are missing, by not being out there all the time?"

"I know we are not catching all the convoys," I said. "Well, maybe we could spend more time out there. In one way, it would be easier if the village was closer. But they would not be as safe."

"That's true," Silver replied. "I also found out they have CIA people in Laos, north of us a ways, monitoring the trail as it comes outta North Vietnam. They are based in Thailand."

"So, they are serious about keeping this thing as closed as possible."

"That seems to be the way it's headed."

"Silver, if that is true, then they are going to start hitting back at whoever they think is doing them damage, where ever they can. That means us. What do you think?"

"You are probably right. Let's set up a long perimeter all the way around us, with sentries some distance out maybe a mile.

"Good idea."

The plan was just in time, for a few days later a young boy came running into the hamlet. He ran to Silver and dropped to his knees, out of breath. He managed a "Beaucoup VC!" and pointed back to the northeast. Silver patted the boy on the shoulder and handed him a canteen of water. We immediately mobilized, and headed out double time. About an hour later, a young man popped out of the trees and motioned for us to stop and be quiet. We crawled up to the edge of a ridge and saw a large patrol of VC coming up a trail below us, practicing as much stealth as a large group of men could manage. We fanned our troops out and moved down trail on either side, just out of sight. We caught them at the base of a hill as they came down. They had little cover, and we cut them to pieces. We could not afford stragglers getting free and telling what happened for our own security. We moved the bodies off the trail and disposed of them, leaving no trace. The Degar men didn't like doing this, something in their beliefs about not touching dead bodies, because evil spirits possess them when they die. We convinced them that it was necessary, so the enemy would not be able to link it back to their village and families. This made it worth doing, as they were very protective. We had to repeat this one other time some weeks afterward.

My life in the village was very enjoyable, I felt very much at ease with these people. I had always enjoyed a simple life, and this was, except for the occasional battle. They soon became like family. I loved going to the river and watching the children swim and play. Their carelessness about nudity was amazing to me, especially having grown up in post-WWII America and the mentality of the 1950's. I found their manner of dress practical and logical. They didn't have the hang-ups about their bodies like the people at home did.

One day as I lay relaxing in the sun, I

looked up the river and looked at the route it had taken as it wandered its way down through the country. I realized it seemed to do a semi-circle around the village. I got up and walked upstream, keeping note of the location of the village site as I followed the stream bed. After a short walk, I realized we were above the village about a quarter mile from it. I chuckled to myself.

I turned and walked straight to the village. As I entered the village, I spotted Silver sitting with a group of men. I walked over to him.

"You gotta few minutes?" I said.

"Yep."

"Come with me."

We walked back down the path to the bathing spot, then turned and went upstream to the spot where I had stopped before.

"You notice anything particular about this spot, Mr. Silver?"

He frowned. He didn't like being called that. "Nope, not really."

I was elated. I saw something the great Silver didn't see!

"Silver, we are above the village"

He looked puzzled. "So, why does that matter?"

I laughed. "We can run water into the village. The women won't have to carry it all in themselves."

I watched the light bulb above his head start to glow. "Wow, Mr. Boots! That is a great idea! But how do we direct it?"

I laughed again. "Well, all those old Tarzan movies are finally gonna pay off. Remember in his house he used bamboo for water lines? We got beau-coup bamboo."

He laughed. "Let's go talk it over with the men in the village."

As we walked back, I showed him the tentative route the pipeline would have to take to keep the proper fall. He kept looking at me all the way back.

"Boots, what made you think of this?"

"I was raised on a farm. I have irrigated many a field. And I just think along those lines. And those women, they work awfully hard. This would make it easier for them."

"You like being here with them, don't you?"

"Oh, yeah!"

We sat, and Silver explained the idea to the men of the village, pointing to me that it was my idea. It took some time to get the idea across. Finally, an agreement was reached. Next morning, armed with machetes and axes, we headed up the hill. I pointed out the bamboo that I wanted, and set them to cutting it into lengths and opening the its joints. I found a point in the stream where it pooled a bit and a small dam of rocks could be built to raise the water level. I set the first one in place, and we built the dam around it and secured it as much as possible with what we had to work with. We did not dam the stream yet, or raise the water level. I had marked the path, and the men followed it. In a few places we had to raise the bamboo troughs on crossed stilts to keep the level of flow. Other times we had to move some earth and stone to keep it level.

Late on the third day we entered the village. At the point we stopped, the end trough was about four feet off the ground. I directed our workers to dig a crude ditch or canal from the village, and point it downhill toward the river again in hopes the water would go full circle. We had shown four men how to dam the stream and raise the water level. They were sent back to the start of the pipeline with instructions to start the water. The whole village came and stood around the end of the pipeline. An hour went by, then another half hour. Then two hours. I was starting to sweat. Had something gone wrong? Did it break? It should be here by now. Then, suddenly, a gurgle. Then a trickle. Then a stream. Then the stream got stronger. Water splashed off the big rock below the fall, and then ran down the shallow ditch, soaking its way through the village! A shout went up. Children jumped into the waterfall, and people came and drank, some bringing containers to fill. That night there was a celebration in the village. The rice wine was brought out, and a feast was prepared. I don't think I was ever so satisfied in my life about something I had accomplished, and to this day it makes feel good to remember that day over 50 years ago. Silver came and shook my hand. "Boots, that was remarkable! I am proud to know you and to have you as my partner!" With that, my chest stuck out a bit farther.

My little friend Sui spent many nights lying in my arms. We slept together much of the time, but still I couldn't bring myself to take the relationship farther. There was such an innocence with her, that although I couldn't help being attracted to her, and my natural male urges were sometimes hard to suppress, I just couldn't feel right about it. She would spend endless time talking to me, sometimes very animated, sometimes very quiet. I listened respectfully, trying to be aware of everything in her manners. Indeed, if Vietnam taught me anything, it taught me to be aware. She smiled a lot, and when she would look at me and smile, I must confess, my heart would just melt. I think that I fell in love with her early on. I watched her nimble hands in her daily tasks. It seemed as if they had a brain of their own. She always smelled so good. I wondered how. There were no Woolworth stores with perfume counters in central highlands of Vietnam in the early 60's. Finally, one day she was sitting and talking to me, and I reached out and took her hands and stopped her. I then leaned in and sniffed her neck and shoulder. I then pointed to my nose and made pleasant gestures and smiled. Then I touched each side of my head, and made a puzzled face, and pointed at her neck and my nose alternately. She stopped and looked at me very carefully. Then smiled, and she was gone. I waited, hoping I had done nothing to offend her. I spent a lot of my time those days wondering if I offended these people. Language is such a bitch some time.

Then she was back, with some flowers and a small bag of something that looked like my Grandma's snuff, only kinda pasty. She opened the bag, and put her fingers into it and touched them to her neck and breasts, then offered herself to my nose. It was very nice, sweet and flowery. She then took the flower, pinched out the inside, and offered it to me and I smelled it. Nice, but not as strong. She made motions of putting it into the bag, but did not. I assumed there must be more to the process, but my question was answered.

One evening we were sitting in my hut at sundown. I missed my music. I grew up with the advent of rock and roll - Elvis, Jerry Lee, Chuck, Buddy, and all the boys. She was doing some small task - I don't remember what. I started to sing Elvis's song "Love Me Tender". As I sang, she stopped what she was doing and looked at me. I turned and sang to her, smiling as I did. As I sang, tears formed in her eyes and ran down her cheeks. She looked at me with her innocent face as soft and warm as I had ever seen. When I finished she rose up and put her arms around my neck and hugged me very tightly, then let me go, patted my hand, and disappeared into the evening. A few minutes later she was back two young children. Two little girls. I had seen them but didn't know who they were. She made sounds and motions for me to sing again, and they all sat around me, looking attentively. I thought of another song I liked of Elvis's, "Ol' Shep", about a dog. I sat down in front of them, and sang what I knew of it even adding some words of my own at times. As you may know, the song is a sad song, about a dog dying. As I sang, I noticed all my audience was in tears. This puzzled me. They understood almost no English, but obviously the message came through. Here was the heart of communication. After that, I decided to change the mood. Next up was "You Ain't Nothin' But A Hound Dog", and then "Heartbreak Hotel". I got up and did my best Elvis impersonation. I shook and jumped and wiggled until my audience was in hysterics. We talked for a few minutes, then sleepy eyes began to close. So the girls were taken back to where they came from, and soon Sui was back, and we drifted into dreamland together.

We awoke early next morning. I sat up and watched as her beautiful sleepy face came to life. She smiled and was gone. After a while she was back with food and water. We had our morning meal. I put my bowl down and said, "Sui, you sing your song." I pointed to her mouth and sang a bar of "Love Me Tender" so she would understand. She smiled shyly and shook her head no. "Oh Please, Sui!" I said, "Boots sing, Sui sing!" pointing to each of us respectively.

She sat quietly. Then this beautiful, very high, lilting voice began to unfold a song. I listened with all my might. It was a strange language, a different style of music. Her face was almost entranced as she sang. At times soft tears would run down her cheeks. I listened until she finished. I smiled and hugged her, then kissed her on the forehead. I had no idea what may happen with this girl, but she was awesome, like no one I had ever known. I had no idea what the song was about, but it was spellbinding. Our relationship was becoming more than I cared to think about. I wasn't stupid. I knew if I continued to live at some point I would have to leave. What then? I didn't want to think about that at all.

CHAPTER 7

It was about 1100 hours on some day of the week, I never knew which one. Calendars didn't seem important anymore. We heard choppers. In a minute or less, three of them passed over, heading south, maybe southwest a bit. I looked at Silver, he looked at me. These were the new choppers, the ones that would later be called Huey's by everyone. I had seen one on the ground, but never in the air. But three, they were impressive. They were flying low. All the kids ran into their huts, and the people all appeared to be nervous. Me, I was puzzled by what was going on.

Later that afternoon our little plane landed at the clearing. We were waiting. When it landed, a man in a light colored trousers and a sport shirt stepped out. I recognized him from one of our trips to MAAG-V at Da Nang. I helped the pilot get the cargo out. We had some mail, always welcome, from that imaginary place on the other side of the world. Best of all, my new bow. A 65 lb. pull re-curve Wing Thunderbird. After watching the Yard men with their crossbows, I decided that it would be a real contribution to our time of warfare. My Grandpa Chris had made me a longbow when I was 13 or so. I hunted small game and fish with it as I grew up and I became quite accurate with it. In the next bundle was around 30 arrows and a quiver. I had gotten arrows with target tips but had bought some add-on hunting points. I needed to practice some.

As soon as the little plane had fallen off the mountain and climbed back into the sky, I turned to Silver.

"What was that about?"

"We are supposed to start searching some of the lowland villages and watching for VC activities. It seems there is a large build-up east of us, and they are moving out and attacking ARVN units in company strength. They actually want us to move the village to another location and begin fortification. I hope not. These people have managed to stay secluded for years. I hope they can stay here."

I nodded. "Me too." My thoughts were *I don't want anything to change for them.* But we knew it was getting more dangerous all the time.

After a couple of days practicing with my new bow, my skill returned, and I became more confident as a well. The Degar men thought it was awesome. They handled it as if it was a piece of expensive jewelry. We had found a bank of dirt where a tree had uprooted and fallen, and made it a target for practice. When I offered to let them shoot it, I was impressed with the appreciation they showed. Each in turn was respectful of each other and me. And when they were through, they wiped the bow clean ,and the arrows as well, and returned them to me with smiles and nods of appreciation. God, I had grown to love these people. I had never had brothers, and now I had a village-full. It was a good feeling.

As per our instructions, we went east for a few days. We watched a village for a day and a night, then left. We watched another village, then left. The third one we scored. Late in the afternoon we watched at least fifteen heavily armed men head out down a trail. We followed them. They entered a small encampment with maybe ten more soldiers.

"Something's up." Silver said

I agreed. Next morning, early, they broke

camp. We watched them as they moved to a highway about three miles away. There they set up an ambush.

Silver said, "We need to get in close and see what they are waiting for."

I agreed, "Yes, but, let's not hit them until they attack. They will be totally confused."

We moved in behind them until we were within 50 yards or less. The Yard soldiers were masters at this sort of thing. I moved down to about 30 yards from three VC, just slightly below me and hidden just off the road. I took my bow and strung it and pulled three arrows and stuck them in the ground in front of me. Standing behind a tree I was not visible to the men below me. We sat and an hour went by, then two. Then three. Then down the road came the rumble of trucks. In and out of view, down a hill and up over the next, straining and roaring, not knowing what lay right in front of them. As the first truck rounded the last curve and approached, you could see the two men closest to the road ready themselves. I pulled my first arrow. The first truck went by. As it did, the man stood ready to throw what looked like a grenade. I let my arrow fly. It caught him in the shoulder.

I pulled my next arrow and fitted it, as I did the grenade exploded. Both men were blown up. The other attackers stood to fire at the trucks, at the same time our soldiers opened up on them. One by one, the attackers realized they were being attacked instead of attacking. The AK's opened up, spraying bullets everywhere. I dropped my bow, picked up my carbine, switched it to automatic, and sprayed the roadside below. By then, the trucks had stopped and soldiers were jumping out and shooting. The trucks had been full of ARVN soldiers. I don't know if any VC escaped or not, I doubt it.

When the shooting stopped, Silver yelled, "American soldiers! Hold your fire!" Then he yelled again in Vietnamese, probably the same thing. I motioned for our men to stay down. They did. Silver then stepped into the open, holding his arms up. Down below I saw a Vietnamese soldier step out and wave. Silver walked down the hill and shook hands with the man. Turns out he was a Lieutenant Quan. We had just saved his and his troop's asses, with a handful of little men in breech clouts and khaki shirts that we had obtained for them as uniforms.

We all came out of the jungle and walked

down. I watched our men. They were very wary of the ARVN, the looks that passed between them told me we should move on. I told Silver we were going to find a spot to rest up the road. He nodded and continued his conversation. The men and I walked on up the road to a small stream to relax. My little sniper buddy, Malik, came over and patted my bow and smiled, saying, "Good, good." I nodded and said, "Thank you." I watched him mouth the words, *Thank you.* These guys had such an insatiable desire to learn, it was inspiring! I suppose it was then that I realized that learning came from desire, not from mandate. Setting up a system to educate a people was rather worthless unless the desire to learn could be instilled. Would I have a desire to further myself if I was lucky enough to make it back to that other world? Indeed, that was the way I had started to think of it, the other world....This had become the real world to me. We headed back to our village that afternoon. It was late the next day before we made it back. I dropped my gear, picked up my shower kit and towel, and headed for the falls.

I stood in the cool water, letting it run over my body, letting days of perspiration and grime wash away the smell of blood and gunpowder from my nose, I stood with my eyes closed and thought about the things happening around me almost daily. I felt very alone and confused. This wasn't me, but it was. Then I opened my eyes. Sui was standing right in front of me our bodies almost touching. I looked down at her totally nude body. She reached up and put her arms around my neck and buried her face into my neck, almost as if she sensed my despair. Her legs came up and wrapped around my waist, we sank down into the pool. I looked at her and as softly as possible, I kissed her sweet lips. She kissed me back cautiously, then more fervently. We lay, our bodies intertwined together, for a long time.

It was almost dark before we pulled ourselves apart and walked back up the hill to our humble hooch. I was entirely aware of the giant step we had made. I hoped it wasn't a huge mistake, but I knew now that she wanted it as much as I did, and I couldn't help but think that might make it right. We spent every free moment together from that time forward. Silver noticed right away. He never said anything, but I could tell he was concerned. But no more than I. Our evenings now were like an everlasting honeymoon. I was on a high that I never believed possible.

About 3 weeks went by. We had been out on several reconnaissance trips. We had more skirmishes with VC, and small battles. It seemed as if they were everywhere. We went out one morning to investigate reports of vehicular traffic on a northern part of the trail. It seems that North Vietnam had put a special division of men to work expanding the trail. We had to go north of our regular area of work for about a day. We saw signs of vehicles of some sort, but had given up and were heading back. We were in a particularly dense part of jungle when suddenly the men just froze. About that time a shot rang out. One of our men yelled and went down. I was searching the jungle when I sensed someone behind me. I turned to see a machete-type blade flashing by me. It almost missed, just barely slicing a small cut in my right buttock. I raised my .45 and fired at point-blank range.

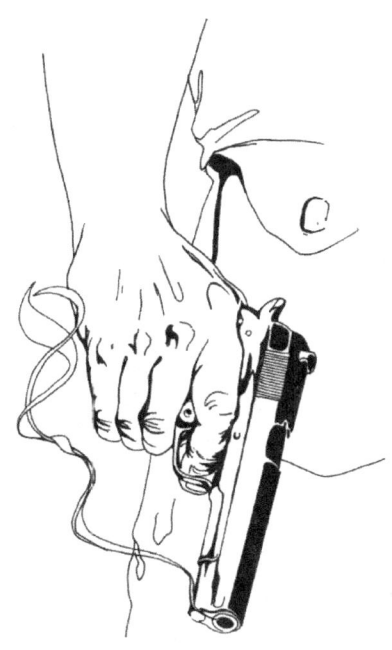

I looked at the person as the body went down. I was surprised to see an almost pretty Vietnamese woman, she couldn't have been much over twenty years or so of age. My heart just jumped, and another bullet went by. I came back to focus, realizing the man behind me had been hit. It seemed the area to the right of the trail was the prime source of the bullets, so I pulled the M2 up and fired it fully auto in that direction. Everyone was shooting. It seemed like everything was in slow motion, like a dream, a really bad dream. Then it was quiet, everything was quiet, except cries and moans.

I looked around. Silver was out about 25 yards or so in front, still standing with gun in hand. I looked down at the dead woman, and suddenly my stomach came up. Everything I had eaten for hours, which wasn't much. I finally got myself together.

She was lying on her back, her eyes still open, blood on her face and oozing out of her body. I felt hard, cold anger, but not at her. I knelt over her. I took her shirt and wiped her face clean. I closed her eyes and patted her hand and touched her face. I looked at her. Someone's daughter, someone's sister, maybe someone's girl or wife. It was all so stupid! My voice cracked and tears came to my eyes, and I said, "I'm sorry, sweetheart, I really am. I am not mad at you, I bear you no malice." I looked up. Silver and two of the men were looking down at me. He said, "We gotta go!"

We lost five men that day. Three dead, two wounded. One was my little sniper buddy, Malik. He had a bullet hole in his leg. It went clean through, but he would survive. The Degar don't believe in carrying out their dead, but we convinced them to do it. I backed up to my buddy, and motioned him onto my back. We walked steady for a couple of hours. We stopped and treated wounds and spent the night in the jungle. But it was a pretty sleepless night. At dawn we headed out. We walked all day, carrying the wounded and dead, taking turns.

It was almost sundown when we saw the smoke. Our hearts sunk, we knew what it was. We left our dead and wounded, and we ran straight for the village. We had our weapons at ready when we came out of the jungle at the edge of the clearing. It was the worst we could imagine. Bodies lay everywhere. Most of the buildings were burned or mostly burned. Total devastation. I started looking for Sui. I saw one of the young girls that had been in my audience, she had been shot, I will not say where. Why? How could human beings be so horrible? Children.....

I kept looking. As I made my way to where my hooch had stood, I saw her lying just outside of it on her stomach. I knelt down. I gently picked her up and turned her over into my lap and the cradle of my arm. I smoothed her hair away from her face. I wiped her face clean. I knocked the dust and dirt off her body. I properly arranged the little bit of clothing she wore. I sat there rocking the small body in my arms, and then the floodgates opened, and I cried like I had never cried in my life. My tears fell on her face and breasts. All the pain and terror of the last two days came out. I felt loss, and hurt, and anger, and rage. I had never hated anyone really, but I felt consumed with hate for the first time in my life. There was no fairness in the world. I held Sui for an unknown amount of time, leaning over her with my face against that sweet face, crying.

A touch on my shoulder brought me to consciousness. It was her brother, Malik. He knelt beside me and we cried together. Finally, he sat up. He reached over and touched my shoulder and said, "Boots, we go, kill VC."

I wiped the tears from my eyes. "Yes, little brother, we go kill VC!"

I picked Sui up in my arms and carried her out to the pile of bodies that were being laid out. By then a few people were starting to come in out of the jungle. Silver met me about that time. He looked at the lifeless body in my arms. He looked down, then reached out and touched her face. He looked at me. I think I saw a tear on that carved face of his.

"I don't know what to say, Boots. I know you cared a lot for her. That was plain to see. And she cared for you. I am so very sorry."

"You can say that we are going to get those

bastards. I want them to pay!"

"Yeah, don't worry. We are going, you can count on it."

I thought for a few minutes about placing Sui in the mass grave we were digging. Then I picked her up again and carried her back to where our little house had stood. Just outside was a big tree, where we had sat for long periods of time. She would talk and I would listen, and I would talk and she would listen.

I think back now, years later, would it not be an awesome thing if more couples did that?

I got a trenching tool that had survived the fire, and dug a grave as deeply as I was able. From inside I found remains of an old military blanket, and part of a mummy bag. I carefully wrapped her little body, and put her in the bag, and lay her in the grave. I took one last look at the face I had grown to love, then carefully covered it and filled the grave. I patted it down, and found as many rocks as I could, and stacked them over her to keep the scavengers out. I knelt over her and cried unashamedly. Finally I stood and said, "Goodbye Sui, I will never forget you."

I never have.

CHAPTER 8

I turned toward the village and allowed my rage and anger to push my hurt and sorrow aside for the business at hand. The next days were a blur of travel. Searches following a cold trail. My buddy Malik was by my side. Even with his injured leg he kept up. No one talked, words were not necessary. We entered villages, careful to not be cruel. We looked for any sign of VC everywhere. We had a few skirmishes, nothing major. We continued north along the Laotian border, at some point we gave up on the trail. Finally, along a another road we came to a border with Laos, and Silver said,

"We are getting close to North Vietnam, it's time to turn back."

So, turn back we did, I think we all felt a sense of failure, but by then we were not even sure, where are who killed our people, it was time to turn back.

Later that day Silver talked to our leaders. He basically told them that we would go back and we would hunt the VC, that we had lost the ones that hurt our people, indeed, they may still be back there somewhere. By now, the emotion had subsided, and they were ready to go back. We moved back into South Vietnam.

We traveled some main roads. Finally, we turned back to the west. The next morning we broke camp early. We had gone maybe a mile when we came upon an ARVN company breaking camp. We stopped, and Silver talked to the officer in charge. They were headed in the same direction we were going. We went on ahead to keep the two parties apart - the Yard men did not like the ARVN, and we didn't want an incident. About a mile ahead we turned off the road onto a trail heading west toward the village.

We had gone about fifty yards when suddenly all hell broke loose! Shots were fired, and men were running out of the jungles with machetes. We were sitting ducks. We ducked into the jungle. I couldn't get a handle on how many were attacking or from where. I picked my targets in the heavy foliage, sometimes hitting, sometimes not. Men were screaming. Then I heard small arms from the road; the ARVN had caught up. I fired at a body running away then turned to see Silver about thirty feet away. As I turned, a bullet whistled by my ear, so close

I could feel it. I saw Silver jerk, and a red spot appeared on his chest. He looked at me almost in disbelief, then there it was, one of the little Silver half smiles, the lights in his eyes slowly went out and he sunk to the ground.

I was stunned! Not Silver! I ran to his side, and kneeled down, but he was gone. I sat motionless beside him. Tears wouldn't come for him. Instead, I felt an ache way down deep, a loss. What do I do now, without him? I could see no way.

The men came and stood around, quietly, respectfully. Then, almost as a man, they lowered to their knees and bowed their heads for a long moment, then stood and walked away. The young ARVN officers arrived. He spoke some English. He expressed his condolences. I asked him if he could take Silver's body back to the nearest military station. He said he would, and two soldiers came to get him. I waved them off. I bent down and picked him up and carried him down the trail to the road. I laid him in the back of the truck, closed his eyes, and took his hand.

"Goodbye, my friend. Damn you for leaving

me in a mess like this! You got me into this! I tried to learn everything you taught me, but I know it is only maybe a tenth of what you know. Life is going to get hard now. Silver, I'll never forget you. I hope we meet again in another life somewhere. Go rest now, you have fought enough battles. I will find out where you are sleeping and come see you. Goodbye for now!"

I turned and all my Montagnard soldiers were standing around me, looking at me for instructions. *Oh my God, I can't let them down! I can't let them see my confusion.*

I pointed back toward the trail and the long road home. I said, "We go." and headed up the path.

There were only twelve of us now, four of which had pretty serious wounds. I paired each wounded man with two uninjured men with instructions to help. We buried the dead and started home - to a home that was really not there anymore.

At this point, I will have to apologize to those of you hearing to my story. I don't remember much of what happened the next few days. My thoughts and feelings were in such turmoil that somehow the hours and the days went by in a blur.

We made it back to the burned-out village, but we were no longer a fighting force. Only a handful of people had survived the massacre, and not much remained from the last battles in which we fought. I knew it was over here, but how do I end it? How do I tell these people it's over? Would they have been better off if we had never been here? It was hard to say, it might have happened anyway.

The next morning I came to the center of the village and waited for the handful of people to gather. One of the men knew just a smattering of English. I motioned him to come over. I told him to talk for me. I said to them, "Boots must go home. I am sorry. You have been my family, but I must leave you. I will never forget you. I hope you will be safe and make new homes. I thank you for helping me and making me a member of you village." I tapped the bracelet on my wrist. "For now, Goodbye."

I had little to carry except my weapons and pack. I asked for a guide to go to Dak To. A young man stepped forward. We turned and I walked away from a chapter out of the pages of my life that was filled with more feeling than I was able to sort out at the moment. I stopped at Sui's grave, then headed down the trail to the east.

We walked all that day. We slept that night, but my sleep was full of dreams and discomfort. The next day as we walked a trail on a high ridge looking over a valley to the east, my thoughts were about what I was going to do now. Confusion clouded my mind, so clouded that I didn't even see them until it was too late.

As we rounded a bend just past a big tree, five VC soldiers stood in a semicircle surrounding us, their weapons leveled at us.

Before I could move, they moved in, striking me mid-body with a couple of rifle butts. I went down, and I couldn't get my breath. I tried to get up. My rage came back, and I struggled to rise. As I did a barrel of an AK was stuck into my neck. They were shouting something I didn't understand. I could hear myself yelling back, cursing them. I was struck again, this time in the back. I went down again. Someone kicked me in the neck, and again in the back. This time I was down. *Oh God, this it, I'm dead!*

My heart sank. I was sick at my stomach. Everything went black for a minute. When I came to my hands were tied. I was pulled to my feet and half-dragged up the trail. I was struck numerous times, but I didn't really feel it anymore. I felt like a dead man walking.

We continued walking until well after dark. I remembered thinking, *Get away, don't let them keep you prisoner. They will torture you, then kill you when they find out you are of no value. At least take out one or two of them. Bide your time.* Silver and I had talked about it. I quit protesting and just obediently walked as slowly as they would let me. I would stumble and fall occasionally, not enough to make them think I couldn't make it, because then they would kill me for sure. I would try to slow them down, hoping for a chance to escape.

As we came to a stop, it was apparent we were going to stop for a while. I watched my opportunities. With my hands tied in front of me I only had one chance. I caught one guy unaware. I planted a kick to his groin as he went down. I grabbed his AK and one-handed it, with both hands. Just as I was about to pull the trigger, the lights went out. Some one was watching me.

I awoke several hours later. My head and the back of my neck hurt profusely. I tried to touch my head with my hand. I realized that it wouldn't move and looked over. They had taken a long piece of bamboo and tied it across my shoulders and tied my wrists to it at the ends. I would look like a walking cross. They were taking no chances.

Soon, everyone was awake. One brought me a cup of rice and some water. My first thought was to kick him in the face, but decided it would be wiser to keep them guessing and play along until a real opportunity arose. I took it, and looked him in the eye and said a real heartfelt "Thank you."

He didn't look very trusting. I wondered if he was the one I had kicked.

Soon, I was pulled to my feet, and the trek started again. I had to admire these guys. They were serious. They moved all day on a handful of rice. They jerked me around pretty good. I didn't have to fake falling very much. I did it pretty regularly. Try it sometime, tie a pole across your shoulders and try walking in the woods on rough terrain. Not only is your balance off, but things grab your arms unexpectedly.

By the time we stopped the second day I was pretty well whipped. I was in survival mode, looking for opportunities, hoping - no, *dreaming* - of rescue. By the third day, hope of rescue was diminishing. I was getting too far north. My hands were aching terribly; the circulation was cut off to much. I finally got someone to look, my hands were blue. They sat me down and retied me. Not any looser, but it didn't cut off my circulation anymore.

I did mental calculations, watching the sun and moon. I judged us to be somewhere along the Laos-Vietnam border, but I could only guess which side. I wondered where they were taking me. They seemed to think it a good idea to keep me going. I knew there was a good reward for an American Soldier, but I was not in uniform. I had no ID or dog tags. I knew what I should do according to the uniform code of military conduct as a prisoner. But I decided to not play that card. If I could convince them I was a civilian, and worth a reward, that might get me out alive. It could also get me shot as a spy. Shit! They would probably kill me anyway, so why not give them nothing. I remembered Silver and I talking about being social workers, and decided that was the way to go. Now, to just stay alive one more day.

That night one of my captors brought me my rice ball and water. He said, "You name."

I looked at him, and pointed to myself with a nervous look (which wasn't hard to fake), "I am Cowboy!"

He chuckled. "You Cowboy?"

I nodded. He turned to his buddies and said something in Vietnamese. Everyone had a good laugh. This was good, lighten the mood.

He asked, "Where you from?" He spoke understandable English.

I said, "Texas."

He laughed again and turned   and repeated, "Texas." Again a laugh. He went away and joined his friends. I took advantage of that to rest and relax my beat-up body. I was surprised they had not taken my boots. I guess my size 12 seemed somewhat useless to them. I managed to doze off. I was jerked awake by one of them yanking my rope, yelling, "Come, Texas!"

Our fourth day of travel went about the same as the other three, only they were not beating me anymore. But it was rigorous just trying to keep up. With my arms outstretched my shoulders and back ached constantly. My hands felt like wood. I didn't know if I would ever regain use of them, but I had stayed alive another day. I have to tell this part - believe me it isn't easy, but you have to know - they didn't stop for bathroom breaks. I had shit my pants, and urinated several times. I was a mess.

We had reached a fairly fast-flowing stream at the end of the fourth day. I made motions and told them I wanted to go in the stream, asking over and over. Finally, I just started walking to the stream. I stopped and looked back. Two of them had raised their weapons. I just shook my head, and turned to the water. At least I could die clean. I walked into the water about waist-deep, and moved around a bit, squatting several times to let the water get inside my clothes. Finally, I ducked my head under and shook my head. I was still alive, no one had shot me. I felt better. I walked out of the water, and directly back to them, stopping just short, and said, "Thank you," and bowed from the waist, a deep long bow. I then sat down against a rock, and leaned back and closed my eyes. I won that one! I was given my meager allotment of food, and I slept.

I awoke, before dawn, the next morning. I took the time to try to loosen my bonds when no one was looking. It didn't work. I thought if I could get loose I might be able to sneak away. I had always been good in the woods. Maybe later.

I rested. Soon they woke, and Day Five began. As the morning progressed, we came down off the mountains into a valley. I could see rice paddies. As we walked through them, the mosquitoes started to swarm us. Soon my hands and arms were covered. I couldn't even swat. The pain was excruciating. I remembered the horses and pigs back home, rolling in the mud for protection. I thought, *it couldn't hurt!* I watched for a bare spot of ground, sufficiently muddy and not too grassy, and just fell forward face first, holding my breath. I rolled my face into the mud, and rolled my hands as best I could, but that time they were dragging me up. I shook the mud from my nose and eyes, and said, "Thank you." It might have helped some, I'm not sure, but the mud seemed to soothe the burning.

We traveled several hours through the rice paddies. I saw a village, a small one, at least twice. I wondered, *were these people friendly to Americans, or were they VC villages?* It didn't matter, we never stopped. Day five ended without further incident.

Just before dark, we climbed up into the hills again. The mosquitoes were not as bad as before. My face and neck and ears had suffered, as had my hands. After eating and resting, I remembered the evening with Sui, the first time I had sung to her. It had been a mood changer. I couldn't help wondering what reaction my captors might have. So after conjuring up all my courage, I waited until all were fed and sitting relaxed. I started low, in my best Elvis voice,

"Love me Tender, Love me true, all my dreams fulfilled. For my darling, I love you, and I always will."

I sang the chorus and another verse, and when I quit, I looked up. They were all looking at me, eyes wide open, with a look of wonder on their faces. The one that had originally talked to me got came over to me. He squatted before me.

"Cowboy, more!"

I looked at him and grinned and shook my head. Next I did my rendition of "Home on the Range." They liked that. Then I did "Amazing Grace". After that, I tipped my head and closed my eyes. There were several grunts and sighs. Then it was quiet.

Day Six was all uphill. Finally, after I had fallen half a dozen times, they stopped. A conference was held. The leader came and while two held their weapons on me - which I might say was a bit unnerving they cut my arms loose and took the bamboo off my shoulders. They then tied a rope around my hands, binding them, then hooked a lead rope to my hands. I looked each of them in the eyes and said to each a solemn, "Thank you."

We made more miles that day. I didn't try to slow them down. I didn't want that bamboo pole back on my neck, so I don't know for sure who won that round. Later that day, when we stopped for the evening, the pole - or another one - came back. They couldn't risk me getting loose at night. The next morning, however, they removed it again, and retied my hands. It wasn't ideal, but it was better than before.

Day Seven. We traveled 'til about mid-afternoon. As we walked into a village of about a hundred or so people, the children ran alongside us. I think I may have been the first white person they had ever seen. I was taken to a small hut in the center of the village and led inside. Two of the men sat down to watch me. I sat down on the bamboo mat. It felt strangely comfortable and familiar. Shortly I was brought a bowl of water, then around evening a middle-aged woman, her teeth all black from betal nut, brought me rice and cabbage, and maybe chicken. It was delicious. The first real food I had eaten in days. I thought about it. I didn't remember how many days, actually. It all seemed surreal. It had maybe only been a week or so since my life had blown up. And yet, all my senses were all on edge. I was aware of everything going on around me. I was even trying to figure out the thoughts of these men that had me captive. I was busy gauging my body's ability to do what it needed to do to survive. I doubt that if I had looked at myself in a mirror that I would have recognized me. Whatever turn this road was to bring, I wanted to be leaning into it at the proper time. It was not the time to high side for any reason.

I drifted to sleep, and dreamed. Sui was sitting beside me in the moonlight, singing her beautiful song. As I awoke, like normal, she was gone. I wiped the tears from my eyes. I was ready to face another day.

It was late in the morning when we left the village. After another good meal I felt I had regained some of my strength. My thoughts turned again to escape, but this time it must be planned. I would do nothing to alert my captors until the moment arrived.

Day Eight took us through beautiful mountain valleys. As we stopped for a break and some water, I asked the leader again,

"Laos?" and looked around, "Vietnam?"

He just smiled and shook his head. He wasn't saying. I just shrugged my shoulders.

We kept north, only deviating to go around a mountain or cross a stream. It was still hot, day and night, but I had become used to it. The nights were better. If the situation had been different, I would have probably enjoyed the scenery. I wondered how long it would stay this way. I had heard that a little farther south the Air Force was spraying chemicals on the jungle to defoliate it, so the VC couldn't hide. I knew that America's war machine was relentless. I had seen pictures of Europe during the World Wars, I and II, and the Islands of the Pacific. If it got bad enough, and lasted long enough, there would be nothing left of this beautiful place. I wondered if I would live to see it. I had to put that out of my head!

We walked on, farther and farther from everything that I knew and felt safe with. All I had was me to rely on now! That evening, we stopped and ate our rations. The captors seemed more relaxed this evening.

After we ate, Number One walked over. "You sing?"

I looked around. What could I sing? I didn't know a lot of songs. Then it hit me. I was curious what their reaction would be. I stood up and brought my self to a position of Attention, as much as I could with my hands tied.

I took a deep breath, and....*"Oooh say, can you see? By the dawns early light! What so proudly we hailed....."*

I probably didn't do it justice, and I'm sure I missed some words, but when I finished, I sat down with tears in my eyes and on my cheeks. All the men sat very quietly. The two came over, they said "Cam On," or something like that. I believed it to be *thank you*. Each of them took my hand for just a moment. They looked almost sad. Maybe they knew something I didn't.

Day Nine was a beautiful day. The jungle was alive with birds in song, the air was fresh. We walked until mid-day, broke for a few minutes, then resumed. My captors talked a lot during the day. They seemed a bit excited. About mid-afternoon, we stopped and they put a pole across my shoulders again and tied me to it. They seemed a bit disconcerted. I didn't understand, but we were walking on a well-used road, so it wasn't too difficult. About an hour later, we walked into a sizeable village. As we walked in, the mood of the people was more hostile, and the looks toward me were definitely nasty. We approached the center of the village. As we did, a man stepped out of a hut. Oh shit. He was wearing a NVA uniform. We had reached the end of the journey.

A rifle butt slammed into my shoulders, and I went to my knees. My captors no longer looked sad or friendly.

The officer, a Lieutenant, spoke. "Good afternoon. I am Lieutenant Tran. What is your name?"

I had prepared myself for this.

"Folks call me Cowboy, sir."

He looked at me. "No, I want your full name!" His English was flawless.

"Well, my full name is Tex Randolph Rogers, Sir."

"You are lying to me!"

"Oh, no, sir!"

He looked past me, and another rifle butt

hit me this time over the kidneys. I went all the way down with that.

"Now, what is your name, your rank, and your branch of military?"

I lay still, moaning. I had to stick with this story, regardless. I said, "Tex Randolph Rogers, sir. I have no rank, I am not in any military."

The lieutenant looked at me. He said, "You think about this. We will see tomorrow."

I was picked up and carried over to a cage. It was made out of bamboo. It looked to be about four feet wide and four feet high. They took the bamboo pole off of my shoulders and pushed me inside, rather forcefully. My face hit the bamboo, cutting it, mainly because not enough feeling had returned to my hands and arms for me to catch myself. I fell on my side. I lay for a few minutes, allowing the pain in my back to lessen to some degree. I wiped my bleeding face on my sleeve and felt it gingerly. It was only superficial. I lay for some time, and either passed out or dozed off, I'm not sure which.

When I came to, I was very thirsty. I looked around. There were no guards visible. I shook the cage. It didn't shake very much. I kicked at the door. It didn't budge. This thing was solid. I inspected all the wraps of bamboo stripping, it was all tight. I fell back. A small pit of nausea eased up from my stomach, caused from the fear and hopelessness that I felt. No one came that night, no food, no water. I sat in the darkness, totally alone.

Next morning, shortly after sun up, the lieutenant and his posse arrived.

"Mr. Tex, are you still sure that is your real name?"

"Yes, sir."

"If you are not in the military, why do you call everyone 'Sir'?"

"Well, that's the way my momma and daddy brought me up. They taught me to be polite!"

"Where are you from, Tex?"

"I am from Texas, sir."

"What city in Texas?"

"It weren't no city, sir, it was just a small town. It was called Smithville."

"How long you been in Vietnam?"

"About a month, sir." I tried to look very fearful all the time I was talking to him and to be very fearful, no bravado.

"What are you doing here?"

"My school sent me here, to study the Montagnard People."

He snorted, "Why you want to study the Moi?" He almost spit the word, as if it left a bad taste in his mouth.

"The school sent me and my professor to study their culture. I was mostly to just help him. The school studies a different primitive people every year."

"What school you go to?"

"Why, the University of Texas in Austin, sir. Sir, may I have some water? I am awful thirsty."

"Of course you may."

He motioned and said something Vietnamese. A man approached with a large pot of water, but instead of giving me a drink, he threw it in my face. I was not expecting it. It strangled me and went up my nose. I coughed and snorted water out of my nose.

He laughed. "You still thirsty Tex?"

I didn't answer.

"I don't believe you, Tex. I think you Special Forces, sent here to kill VC."

"No, sir! I don't want to kill anybody! I don't believe in killin'!"

With that, he walked away with his posse in tow. I lay there for several minutes. I sucked as much water as possible out of the wet shirt. It wasn't much though. Later, a group of small boys gathered around. They watched me a while then one picked up a small stone. He threw it, hitting the back of my hand.

"Ouch, why did you do that, you little beggar?"

They laughed, and all of them started pelting me with stones and small clods of dirt. I protected my face and eyes, but they nailed me some good ones. Finally, an older woman saw them and yelled at them and made them leave. She turned and yelled at me and said a bunch of stuff in Vietnamese, then made a gesture by sticking her posterior at me and turning and sticking her pelvis at me. I am pretty sure it was meant to be obscene.

I sat and nursed the pelt marks from the rocks and such. My thoughts turned to the kids. They react the same way the adults do. They see the adults hate and cause pain, then it is alright for them to do the same thing. I remembered when I was a kid and we were fighting Japan during WWII they were made to look subhuman, and as kids we feared and hated them. This was no different. This was obviously not going to be pleasant, to say the least.

CHAPTER 9

Again, night approached with still no food or water. I was starting to feel very weak. I decided they were going to do this to soften me up. But I knew I could never deviate from my story, not for a moment. It was a good story, it was believable.

All night long my intestines growled and rolled. My stomached burned, and small bouts of nausea rolled over me, my lips and throat were parched. I would have sold my soul for a sip of water. My mind wandered uncontrollably, thinking of all the things that I loved to drink and eat. Images of cold, wet, icy cans of Pepsi-Cola danced through my mind, more beautiful than the Rockettes dancing on stage at Radio City Music Hall. There was very little sleep that night.

As the approaching sun started to break the darkness, I waited, hoping today would be better than yesterday. Dawn broke. I had dozed for a moment in the predawn darkness. A lone hen was scratching about a foot or so from the side of my cage. *Could I eat a chicken raw?* The thought lingered in my head. But as I was picturing myself devouring the unsuspecting hen, the village started to wake up. There was the smell of fires being started. Women passed by with baskets and large jars. Sleepy-eyed children with their naked little butts wandered by, eyeing me suspiciously, as if I really was a tiger in this cage. I waited. Patience had never been one of my personal virtues. Smells of food being cooked drifted around me, adding to my misery. An hour, maybe less, slipped by. A woman approached. Not young, not old, but certainly used up looking. She approached me with a small bowl of rice and something I assumed was boiled cabbage with fish sauce dripped over it, and a container of water. She set it just outside my bars and turned quickly and walked away. I called after her, "Thank you."

I reached through the bars for the water first. I picked   it up and started to drink, thinking *Slowly, Boots, slowly.* I stopped myself after a few swallows. My stomach heaved for a moment. I thought I would vomit, but I worked to hold it down. Slowly my stomach settled. I then reached for the bowl of food. Being forewarned by my body's reaction to the water, I scooped two fingers full, put it in my mouth, and slowly chewed and swallowed it. I waited. Again the heave from within, and then it settled again. I tried another two fingers, and it went down ok. I slowly ate the entire bowl of food, licking the bowl clean. Only then did I drink more water. I sat very still and leaned against the back wall of the cage. My innards were still unsure of themselves. By the time the lieutenant and his posse arrived, I was thinking maybe I might live after all. I was a bit premature with that thought.

"Good morning, Mr. Tex. Did you enjoy your breakfast? I sorry we did not have any steak and eggs and potatoes like you are used to eating for breakfast in Texas."

"Yes, sir. It was very good, thank you. And thank the lady that prepared it."

"Well, we needed you to be strong today. We need to ask you some important questions."

"All right, sir, I will try to help you all I can."

With that, they unlocked my cage and pulled me out. I tried to stand up, but my joints didn't seem to want to work. I went to my knees for a moment. Two of my captors picked me up, and I was slowly able to stand.

They walked me over to a rope stretched between two trees. They tied one of my arms to a loop and the other to a loop about five feet away, so I was stretched between them. This didn't look good.

The lieutenant said to me, "Tell me again. What is your full name?"

"Tex Randolph Rogers, sir."

I hadn't seen the man approach me from behind with the rattan staff. The next thing I felt was the blistering sting as he swung it across my back. I hung from the ropes and tears came to my eyes. I struggled back to my feet.

"What is your name, rank, and serial number?"

"Sir, I told you. I am not in the military."

Crack! Another strike. This time lower, across my kidneys.

"I don't believe you. Americans only go abroad to kill innocent people."

"No, that is not true, sir! Most Americans are peaceful people!"

Crack! This time across the shoulders. I

was down for the third time.

"Well, Tex, I don't believe you. I went to school in your America. So I am going to have this man punish you until you tell the truth."

Again a crack and the burning pain. I could feel what I thought was blood trickling down my back. Then another, and another. I lost count of how many times he hit me. Finally, nothing. All was dark.

I was awakened by a big splash of water being dumped on me. The lieutenant stood before me.

"Tex, you need to think about this. It is just going to get worse, until you tell me the truth."

Two men untied me and drug me back to my cage and threw me inside. But I was fed that evening, and again the next morning. I guess they wanted to keep me alive until they got what they wanted. I started to try to remember how long had I been here. Three days maybe, three and a half? I didn't think I could stand much more. But I could not under any circumstances change my story.

That day the treatment changed. The men

would come and urinate on me and laugh as they did it. It was sickening. Then pots of excrement were dumped into my cage and onto me. I became their latrine. This went on for a day, then another day. I was afraid to eat or even drink, afraid it would poison me and make me ill. Finally, I thought it was around day five, the morning broke with clouds and thunder. Within thirty minutes or so, the skies opened and rain, blessed rain, poured from the clouds, washing the filth from my body and the cage. I opened my clothing, trying to wash myself. My thighs and butt were chafed and raw from the sweat and the filth. I scrubbed myself until it hurt, then scrubbed some more. My back hurt from the cuts from the rattan. I rolled over and let the water wash over my back. I opened my mouth and drank from my cupped hands. It was delicious. *Thank you God,* I thought. It stopped as quickly as it started, and the sun broke through the clouds, and I dried. My stink was not as bad as before.

A little later I groaned as I saw the lieutenant and his men approach. I pretended to be asleep. The door was opened, a quick kick, then I was drug out.

"Get up, you lying dog. I am through with

you. I am going to shoot you. You are worthless, and now you will die!"

My heart sank. They stood me up and one soldier put his weapon to the side of my head.

"This is your last chance, Mr. Tex. Do you have anything to say?"

I thought about it. Nothing would change. This would be the final outcome anyway. Now no more pain and humiliation.

I nodded. "No, sir, I told you the truth."

"Shoot him."

Bang! Right beside my head. I dropped. What? I am not dead. I looked up. The lieutenant and his men were laughing. They had put a gun to my head, and fired another beside my head. I dropped my head into my hands. I couldn't allow him to see the hate and anger, the rage in my eyes. Not yet! I was thrown back into the cage.

I lay there almost all day. I had trouble moving my legs. My joints hurt, my whole body was wracked in pain, and worse, there was no hope. I was going to die here. I would never see my family, or have a family myself.

For what? To help these backward people? Not enough. I sank into deep remorse. Even if they opened the door right now, I couldn't walk away. All was dark in my mind.

I lay in my cage, exhausted and beaten. My consciousness ebbed. I either slept or passed out. I didn't much care if I died, it wouldn't be so bad. I didn't think I would ever welcome death, I couldn't stand this forever I am not gonna make it anyway. Then I was sitting in the jungle. Silver came and sat down beside me.

"Boots," he said. "If you are gonna beat this thing, you are going to have to stay strong. You are must find something to keep your mind strong. You are better than this. Don't let him control you, remember who you are. Be aware, keep your body strong. Don't let the cage beat you either. It is only made of bamboo!" He smiled at me in that Silver kind of way, then got up and walked away back into the jungle.

I woke up, sweating profusely. My joints were cramped and my legs numb from the confined quarters. I couldn't sit up or lie down straight, but I could ride a bicycle in this position. I rolled onto my back and raised my legs into a riding position and started pedaling. Faster and faster, up hill and downhill, laughing like a crazy man! But that was ok, no one was watching. When I was thoroughly exhausted, I rolled to my stomach and started doing pushups. One and two and three and four! All the way to 50. I was elated. I felt renewed. I'm not dead, but Lieutenant Tran, you are not going to know that, not now anyway. I rolled over, even my own stink couldn't dampen my spirits, and I fell into a deep sleep.

Next morning, I awoke to the sounds of my cage being opened. Someone reached in and grabbed my arm and pulled me out. I kept myself from standing. I knew I could, but I didn't. So the two men dragged me to a big tree. They sat me down on something and pointed their weapons at me. I pretended to not notice, to be ill, forlorn, beaten. In a couple of minutes, here came the lieutenant and his crew with a bunch of ropes.

"Hey, Tex! You got new story to tell me?"

"No, sir. I don't know anything else." I only murmured, almost inaudibly.

"Well, we gonna give you something to make you think."

They started to wrapping a rope around me and my arms pulling my arms back and wrapping tightly all the way down to the wrists. They threw the rope over a limb above me. Two men started to pull, lifting me up from my hands behind me, bending my arms backward, all the while tightening the ropes around my upper arms and cutting off my circulation. It began to hurt the harder they pulled. As they lifted me off the ground, I was becoming delirious. I could hear someone screaming, then I realized it was me. I hung there, out of my mind with pain. I had to get down, I couldn't stand it. My heart was pumping blood into my arms, but it was tied off, it couldn't get back to return. I literally felt that blood was going to pop out of my pores. I was losing my mind, and losing consciousness.

I started yelling. "I tell you, stop! Stop, I tell you! I tell you anything you want to know!"

This had better work. They released the pressure on my arms, but it didn't stop the pain. I started vomiting. Everything inside, then nothing. I passed out.

Several hours later I came back to life. I remembered what I said. Now I had to make it work. Food and water were setting in my cage. But no one else was around. Next morning Lieutenant Tran and his crew arrived early. He brought me out and sat me on a box.

"Ok, tell me everything."

"Lieutenant, let me start with everything I have seen since coming to Vietnam. I arrived at Tan Son Nhut International Airport. Across from the airport is a huge military base. They have hundreds, maybe thousands, of soldiers there. They have a radar building there, and an Air Base with lots of planes and helicopters. When we left Saigon, we went to a place called Ben Hoa. Again soldiers, equipment, planes, helicopters, and another radar unit. It looked like they are expanding. My next stop was Pleiku. Smaller, but growing. They are fortifying the villages up there. Our next stop was Dak To. Again, very small, but growing. It was there that my Professor and I went into a village. I had heard they were spraying chemicals on the jungle, so your soldiers couldn't hide, but I never saw it. They are concerned. With a particular road, called the Ho Chi Minh Trail, wherever that is. That is all I know."

He sat looking at me somewhat in disbelief for at least a minute. "What is your name?"

"Tex Randolph Rogers, sir"

Something hit me hard from the back.

I woke up back in my cage. It felt like my ribs were broken. I could hardly breathe. I lay there for sometime. I got no food that night, but I did have water. I was still alive.

Next morning, I was dragged back out. I was handed my carbine. Why?

Lieutenant Tran said, "Something is wrong with this weapon, will you fix it for me?"

My brain scrambled. If I try to fix it, he will know I'm military. I picked it up awkwardly. I held it up and looked down the barrel, I slid the bolt, nothing inside. I rolled it over, looking at it. I shook my head, "I am sorry, Lieutenant, I don't know much about guns. They said I needed one in the jungle, but I hoped I would never have to use it. I am not a very good shot." I looked straight at him trying to look as helpless as possible.

He shook his head. "I think you are lying." He untied me and said, "My men hate you. They want to kill you. They want to fight you. I told them to go ahead. Defend yourself if you can. At least be a man, instead of a sniveling coward."

I staggered to my feet. The first soldier came at me. I put my arms up to protect my face, he hit me several times. I fell down, moaning. I struggled to my feet. I could fight, but I could not show any skill. Hard to figure what to do. Number Two came out kicking. He nailed me once in the thigh then he spun to kick me again. I caught his leg and twisted, and he went down, yelling. I immediately went to him, saying over and over, "I'm sorry, I'm sorry." I knelt over him, as if I was comforting him. About that time Number Three hit me in the back. I fell over, grimacing and yelling. As he stepped forward to kick me, I planted a kick in his family planning unit. He fell over, and I swung a roundhouse into his face. Then I fell back holding my ribs.

That ended the fight. I was thrown back into my cage. I nursed my injuries the rest of the day.

From my cage sitting in the back and facing forward, all I had to do was turn my head to the left a bit, and I could look through the door of the lieutenant's hut. He had a chair and a bunk and a table. I could see him walking around. Sometimes he would come and stand in the doorway and watch me for long periods of time. I wondered what he was thinking. I would never let him see me watching, though. As with all my captors, I tried to never make eye contact, always trying to never challenge them.

I was fed and watered that evening. Again, that evening, I continued my exercises. This was a must. I would never have survived the days otherwise. I had read stories all my life about survival, but I never knew it meant all your senses, all your abilities, all your strengths working together. The hardest thing to fight was the depression, and the waiting for the next thing to happen. The aloneness - no one to talk to when it got bad.

Starting about Day Seven or so, a little boy would come and squat about four or five feet from my cage, usually earlier in the day, or late in the day. He would squat there for twenty minutes or so. When he did, I would talk to him. At least there was no angry face there. I would talk to him, I would tell him my name - or the name I was using at the time - and ask him his. I would tell him about my life, and just talk to him. He never said a word. He came for three of four days, then never came back. I missed him, and watched for him all the time.

About Day Eight, I was sleeping, when suddenly a barrage of gunfire exploded around me. Pieces of bamboo and dirt struck me in my face and arms. When I was able to regain my senses, I looked up. Three of the soldiers stood around me, they had fired their weapons around and in my cage. They thought it was real funny. To this day, unexpected explosions around me kindles immediate anger. I can't help it.

I jumped up and yelled at them, "You stupid bastards! I hate your sorry asses! Leave me alone! Go away!"

They opened the cage and pulled me out and gave me another beating until I was almost unconscious, then threw me back. I was almost afraid to think past the current minute now. I couldn't see a future. I was hungry. I was filthy. I would not have wanted anyone that I knew to see me like this. I tried not to think of my mother or father. I was embarrassed at myself, to think of anyone seeing me like this. Nothing should ever be caged, not human, or beast. I thought that night, *maybe it was time to die.*

Day Ten or maybe Eleven. I had exercised in small segments all night. People and soldiers were passing through the village. I didn't want to be seen. Next morning a bowl of food and some water, then Lieutenant Tran and his boys.

"OK, Tex. You of no use to us. We let you go. You go home now, ok? No hard feelings."

I couldn't believe my ears. They pulled me out of the cage and pointed down the road I came in on. I turned slowly, not knowing. Ok. I started to walk slowly, dragging my steps, like I was half paralyzed. One, two, three, four. I walked through the village.

Just as I got to the edge of the jungle, a burst of automatic weapons fire. A burst of bullets kicking up dirt around my feet. I turned, fully expecting a bullet. I didn't care, I just wanted it over, two men came out of the jungle. They shoved me with their rifle barrels, poking me hard, all the way back to the cage. They started stringing me back into the ropes again. Lieutenant Tran was saying, "See? How does it feel for someone to lie to you? Not very good. You think about that."

The ropes were tightening, and now the pain. I was raging inside. All I could think of was killing this bastard!

I yelled at him, "You son of a bitch! You better kill me! Cause if I ever get loose, I will kill you!"

"Tex, I thought you not kill people?"

"You are an exception! One can only stand so much. God, I hate you!"

I could hear myself screaming. I wanted to die. I wanted my heart to just stop. I couldn't live anymore.

I woke in my cage, it was dark, I lay on my side, my arms were bloody, my face and head had blood on it. As I opened my eyes, a small snake crawled by. *Please snake, come back and bite me. End all this.*

Hours later, I woke. The sun was up. Lieutenant Tran knelt beside me. I was laying on my chest and shoulder. I hurt too much to move.

"You tell me now."

My anger returned. "You must be stupid or something. You can't even recognize the truth when it is in front of you. I don't know anything, I am what I say, there is nothing else. Stop this shit, kill me! My life is not worth living. You shame me, you shame yourself." I spit at him. "Your people must be better than this, I hope so." I turned my head and back to him. I heard him walk away. I didn't see him for a day. I slept and exercised, and there was food of sorts. I ate and slept.

CHAPTER 10

Day Twelve arrived. The shooting had broken some of the bamboo under me. I was trying to move it around so it didn't stick me, when one piece moved. My hand went through, and I felt around. Something sharp sliced the end of my finger. I felt again. It was metal! I dug around it and finally freed it. I looked around. There was no one watching so I pulled it out. It was the lid of a can, maybe sardines or something. I slid it back into its hole and relaxed.

Later, after dark, after everyone had left me, I pulled it out. I rubbed it on the sand next to my cage, sharpening it. Then I started cutting the bindings on the side of the back of the cage. The metal was flexible, so I had to be careful. It was a slow process, but by early morning I had almost one whole binding almost cut. I couldn't cut it all the way, lest they see it. It would take time. I hoped I had enough.

The lieutenant didn't seem to have time for me that day. The village was busy, more people arriving and then leaving. That night I worked on the second binding. I had looked carefully. I only needed to cut through three to be able to loosen the bars. I stopped and exercised, I sipped water, I sawed on the bindings. By morning the next day, number two was barely holding. Next day, I was pulled from my cage and interrogated again, slapped around some, then put back inside and left again. Third night, I worked on number three. The piece of metal was slowly being broken and was weakening. I prayed for it to hold out.

As I sawed, I planned what I would do if I got free. I would need weapons, some string or rope, something cut with, and shoes of some sort. They had taken my boots upon arrival. I stopped and exercised before dawn, then sawed until almost daylight. I slept.

I was awakened by a bunch of men entering the camp, all heavily armed, I groaned. I didn't need this. They stared at me as they walked by. No one bothered me all day. I was fed twice, which was a rarity. I had lost a bunch of weight. About mid-afternoon, all the men departed as a group. It seemed like they were in a hurry. As night approached it seemed like the village was almost deserted, with only about three or four men. The lieutenant was still here. I ate my food, and waited. It had to be tonight, it had to be after midnight, when the village was asleep.

The lieutenant came out of his hut. He walked over and took out his tool and took a piss right in front of me, smiling as he did. I looked at him. I didn't see what he had to be proud of, at least in that department. I pretended to be ill and very tired, and ignored him. He thought he had beaten me.

Later, I sawed on the bindings some more. Finally, I turned sideways and as quietly as possible I kicked. Nothing. I kicked again. Nothing. I sweated. Again. It moved! I tried the second one. It moved on the first kick, so did the third. I rolled over, and peddled my bicycle, not enough to tire, just to loosen up. Now to wait. The next two or three hours were the longest of my life.

Finally, I could wait no longer. The moon was out, not a full one, but some light at least. I pushed the bars aside and slid between them, slowly, quietly. I stood and looked around, and then I went straight for the lieutenant's hut. I entered quietly. I could see him sleeping on his side, his back to me. He had a small lantern burning. The first thing

I saw was my Filipino machete! I picked it up, and walked to the bedside. I looked down. Hate and anger boiled inside me. Taking the handle in my right hand, I moved up over him, and with my left I turned him on his back. In one brief moment I dropped the blade across his throat. His eyes blinked, trying to adjust to what was happening.

I whispered, "Guess what, Lieutenant Tran? You were right. I was sent here to kill VC and also NVA. I told you, you sorry piece of shit, you should have killed me!"

With that, I dropped my left hand on the back of the blade near the end and pulled it across his neck, almost severing his head. He kicked and gurgled and blood spurted from his jugular. I watched him a few seconds longer, until he stopped moving. His blood pooled on the floor around the bed. "Goodbye, asshole."

I looked for weapons, but none were to be found. A Vietnamese soda can trunk was locked. Maybe there, but I couldn't wait or make any noise. I picked up a rope, probably the one they had used on me, some cord, a couple of empty backpacks. I looked around. Time to leave.

I stepped out into the shadows. I skirted the edge of the village until I hit the road on the south side. I broke into a trot. It hurt my feet something fierce, but I kept it up for as long as I could. I came to a trail and turned east. I walked, being as careful as I could about where I stepped. Sometime before the moon set, I stuck my feet into the back packs and tied them on with the cord. I also used part of it as a belt, to keep my pants from falling off.

I walked until just before dawn. As it was coming light, I found a big leaning tree and climbed into its canopy. I tied my self to a limb. Exhausted, hurting like hell, hungry, thirsty, but *FREE!* Now I had to stay that way, no mistakes.

Dawn came as I drifted into dreamland. I slept for hours. I awoke sometime about midday. I listened for a long time. I was a few yards off the trail. An hour went by, then two. Maybe this trail didn't get a lot of traffic. Maybe they weren't pursuing me. I cautiously climbed down. I kept heading east. The trail seemed to be headed that way. I came to a stream running fast, and I drank from it. I looked around. I took off all my clothes and waded in and scrubbed myself. I was still sore as hell and had lots of cuts and bruises, particularly on my upper arms and back. I washed them anyway, regardless of the pain. I then washed the tattered rags and lay them on a log. I was upstream a bit from the trail. I listened carefully, but heard no one. I pondered this. It was obviously well traveled, where was everyone?

I got dressed, I found some fruit that I had seen the people eat, and ate some. I kept myself from gorging, knowing my stomach might reject it. I started on the trail again. I almost thought I smelled something, and then I heard something. I jumped off the trail, and climbed up an embankment and hid behind a tree. Within a few minutes, about ten or twelve VC walked by, very quiet, no talking. They didn't seem to be looking, just traveling. And they were going the way I had come from. I gave them a few minutes to get out of hearing range. I was surprised they couldn't hear my heart thumping.

I continued on until dawn, seeing no one else. I found more water and some wild green plants. I didn't know what they were, but I had seen them in the market. I needed meat for strength. I found another tree, tied myself in, and slept. I was pretty used up. It must be ninety or a hundred miles to the coast. I needed more rest and more food if I couldn't find anything friendly before then. And then again, how would I know friendly if I saw it? A disconcerting thought. I would not trust anyone. You know what? I still don't, not completely.

I slept again until midday, if you call tied to a tree limb sleeping. But I never forgot, *I am free, and I will stay free! I will not be captured again!* I was still tired, and my feet hurt. Late in the afternoon I came across a trail that was quite old. *I need to rest.* I walked down it and looked back. There was no sign of my passing.

I walked for about twenty minutes when the remains of an old burned-out building came into view. There was lots of junk that the jungle was attempting to bury. I guessed it was from the days of the French. I walked around. A platform was hung on the side of a tree, about 50 feet out in front of the building. I walked around back. The burned remains of some kind of old motorcycle sat there, rusting away, grown up in vines. Wait, about half of a burned tire hung to the wheel on the front. I pulled on it, and it came partially free. I pulled my machete and cut at it, and it came free. I jumped for joy! My new shoes had just arrived! I went around front and found a bench. I put the old tire down and cut it into two pieces. I measured it to my foot, then cut off some more. I went back to the rear of the shack and found some wire. I laced the front together like it was a canoe. I put it on my foot, perfect fit. I measured the back, cut it and turned the back up and laced it so my heel would have a support against its back. Then I did the other one. They were a bit harsh on my feet. My trousers were ripped up the legs anyway so I cut the bottoms off and put the cloth inside. I closed it around my foot and laced it with cord. I got up and walked around. Much better! Walking would be easier.

There was fruit of some kind on a tree nearby, but I didn't recognize it. I watched and waited. Finally a monkey or two happened by. They took one, and I waited. Then they threw it on the ground. Well, that didn't look good. Then another monkey swung down and picked up one and ate it. I picked two or three. Very sweet, kinda persimmony. That was dinner.

I went back inside the old building. A wine bottle caught my eye. I picked it up and pulled the cork. Empty. I smelled the inside. It smelled winey. I stuck it in my bag that I had been using as a shoe. Nothing else of value here.

I walked back to the trail. Still no one. But someone had passed by. They had pissed on a bush, I could smell it. Now, which way did they go? I would go slowly, watching the trail ahead, listening, listening for any sounds in the jungle. Monkeys, birds flying, anything out of the ordinary. Whenever I topped a hill, I would look as far ahead as possible. I would watch for several minutes, then move on as fast as I dared.

Late on the third day I came upon a stream. I was starving. I walked upstream for a short distance. I found a pool created by some rocks partially damming the stream. I refilled my homemade canteen and my wine bottle.

Wait! What was that? A movement in the water. A fish! Fish was food. I took my machete and found a small bamboo about three quarters of an inch thick. I sharpened one end. I watched. The fish moved into shallower water. I watched, then I stabbed at him, and missed. I found him again. I missed again. Ok, now, relax. Take your time. I watched him. Stab! I got him! I held him to the bottom until I could get my hand under him, then carefully lifted him out. Nice. About nine or ten inches long. Enough for a meal.

I cut off his head and fins, and I removed his entrails. I cut off a small piece and put it into my mouth and chewed. Ok, that didn't kill me. I was careful to remove the bones. That was awesome! I drank some water, and lay back on the bank of the stream.

When I awoke it was dark. *Stupid mistake!* What if I had been found? *Gotta watch that though, no more mistakes.* The moon was waxing, so I decided to try some night travel. The country had smoothed into rolling hills and valleys. I could see farther. I walked on, still no lights or signs of civilization. A lonely place. One of my biggest fears was the big cats that called this country home. Without a gun, I would never be able to defend myself. I had seen several in my stay in the highlands. I had seen tiger, and a cat that resembled an American Cougar, except much smaller, maybe 35 or 40 pounds. Also, a small cat with big ears that looked a bit like my aunt's tabby, except much bigger, maybe 30 pounds. Then there was the one that looked like a leopard. Didn't see much of him though, couldn't really describe him.

All this remembering big cats had me checking the bush around me. Don't need anymore paranoia than I already have. I almost walked into a village in the dark. I caught myself just in time. As I skirted it, I came across someone's garden. In the early dawn light I recognized some vegetables and picked me some, stuffing as much into my bag as it would hold. I was starving, I needed food badly. The vegetables helped. I could use some rice or some other starch. I had been able to catch fish from time to time since that first fish, but eating them raw was less than desirable.

One afternoon I came upon another village. I slipped in as close as possible. Most of the people seemed to be in the rice field a ways from the village. I carefully went into one hut. No one was home, so I rummaged around. I found a pot of rice, and some kind of sticky rice cakes that had a porky taste. I took all I could and left the way I came.

After my heart slowed down again, I found a place and sat and ate. It was delicious, but I rationed myself. I had also found a black pair of baggy pants and black shirt and a straw hat back at the village. I waited until night, donned my new clothes, and headed east again.

Roads were not busy at night, so I became bolder. Traveling at night, sleeping in daytime. I had been free for a little over a week, I reckoned. I topped a rise early one morning and in the distance I could see water, like a big lake or something, way to the east. I found a safe place for the day. That day, I went to bed hungry again,

I woke up late in the afternoon and found some wild fruit. As soon as it was dark, I headed for the big lake. Sometime during the night in the wee morning hours a breeze sprang up from the east. Oh! It was salt air, I was getting close to the ocean! I quickened my pace. Sometime just before daylight, I came to the water. As the light became brighter, I could see it was a big bay. But where? Was I to go north or south? I leaned over the water. It was salty, I couldn't drink it. I caught a glimpse of the face in the water. I recoiled. An unkempt, shaggy, bearded face stared back at me.

I sat on a rock near the road for an hour or so. Then I heard people. I slipped back into the bamboo. They were coming this way. I waited. In a few minutes a squad or so of ARVN appeared. Oh, my God, I never thought I would be so happy to see ARVN!

I took off my Vietnamese clothes and stepped out. When they were about seventy-five yards out, I raised my arms and waved, saying, "Hey, Hey!!!"

Then bang, bang! I jumped behind a rock. *Shit, I couldn't get killed now, not after all this!* I started yelling, "Don't shoot! American soldier! Don't shoot! I am American!"

I waited. Then a voice said, "You American?"

I answered, "Yes, yes, I am American!"

The voice answered, "You raise hands, up high. Come out slow."

I held my hands way high and slowly stood up. I stepped out and walked toward the men. All of them were aiming their weapons straight at me. I prayed for no twitchy trigger fingers. As I got close, the squad leader had them lower their weapons.

"What you do here?"

"Long story. You got food or water?"

Someone gave me a canteen. I drink sparingly from it, then handed it back, thanking him. Another gave me a ration. I can't remember what it was, but I ate it. They took me back down the road.

Shortly we came upon a couple of trucks and more men. I asked, "Where is Da Nang?"

He pointed to the south. I loaded up with them. We drove for a time, I can't tell how long. I kept drifting off and waking. We came to the gate at Da Nang in the afternoon. I don't remember too much. Somewhere about that time I can remember American MP's lifting me out of the truck and taking me to an infirmary of sorts. I was stripped of my clothing and a large tub was filled with water, and I was scrubbed. I was told later I had lots of rashes and sores, especially in my groin area. My feet and lower legs were a mess, but much of my back and arms had healed to a degree.

I woke the next morning lying in a

hospital bed, dressed only in a pair of boxer shorts.

Shortly a nurse came in. "Good morning, did you rest well?"

"Yes ma'am. Thank you."

"What can we get for you this morning?"

"Anything to eat ma'am. As long as it won't bite and isn't raw."

She laughed, "It is already on its way. All you talked about all night was food. We gathered you were about starved."

Minutes later, the most delicious meal I had ever eaten arrived. Scrambled eggs, bacon, hash browns, milk, toast and jelly, and a small stack of pancakes with maple syrup. I started eating and immediately my stomach started to churn. *Whoa, slow down*. I would take an occasional bite, then wait, and do it again. The burning in my stomach got somewhat better. I ate some of everything, but when I could eat no more, there seemed to be enough left for another person.

The nurse came back and said, "Don't worry about it, you will get better. It will just take some time."

She was joined by a doctor. He asked a few questions about how long I had been in the bush. I told him three weeks or so, I wasn't real sure about time. He checked my ears and throat and my tongue. Always my tongue. They put some medication on my rashes and my feet, with a small dressing here and there. He said other than being a bit emaciated, I was pretty much OK.

He said, "There is some brass here to talk to you."

"Sure."

He tucked me back into my bunk and left. As he left, a couple of Captains and a Major walked in.

"Good morning, how are you doing?" The major spoke.

"Pretty sure I'm going to live, Sir, thanks to those ARVN."

"MP's said you identified yourself as 'Boots' last evening. Could you help us out a little better than that?"

"Yes Sir, maybe so." I gave him my cover ID and said he needed to contact the CIA in Saigon. I still wasn't sure about giving him my real name. I had been told not to use it. They asked where I had been. I told them I had been part of a two man team in a Montagnard village up on the Laos-Cambodian border, and that our village had been destroyed and my partner subsequently killed, and that I had been captured some three or so weeks ago by VC and imprisoned, and that I had escaped and made my way back until I came across the ARVN.

"Who was your partner?"

"His name was Silver. His body should have been brought here by an ARVN unit sometime ago."

They looked at each other. One said "Didn't know we had any two man teams up there anymore." They looked puzzled.

The major turned and said "Look, you just rest and recuperate. When they release you, I will leave instructions for a place for you to bunk. Thanks, Boots."

"Thank you, Sir. Could you please check on Silver's body? I promised him I would take care of him!"

"I will let you know."

I lay around another day or so. It was about the end of April. I had found a calendar and found out the date. I had no idea. However, on May 1st, or maybe the 2nd, I was in the mess hall when there was a bunch of chatter going on about two Special Forces guys. I asked someone what it was about. He told me that a team of Special Forces were in a village out west of Da Nang. It was a Yard village, and the village was overrun. I think four of them were captured by the VC, and they were hauled off. Shortly, two of them were killed by the VC for some reason, but a Specialist Quinn, and a Sgt. Groom - I think I have the ranks on the right persons - were imprisoned for a time. But for some odd reason, they were released on May 1st, World Communist Day, and allowed to walk back to civilization. Not sure if they made it all the way or if they had been picked up like I was.

I saw them briefly, a couple of days later, and expressed my congratulations to them. I have always wondered if it had been those VC that passed through the village where I was held captive that had captured them. Guess I will never know.

I was soon back to feeling good again, at

least physically. But I was restless. I wanted to see Dan, find out about Silver's body. I thought I would see if I could get a pass. I went to the Major's office. He was not in, but his aide seemed to have no problem with giving me a pass. I went to my locker, picked up my alias ID and went to the flight line. I soon found a plane headed for Saigon, and soon was winging my way south. We made a few stops, finally arriving late morning.

I arrived at Tan Son Nhut about noon, and caught a ride over to the big hanger to have lunch. Being a Saturday, it was cook your own t-bone day. I hadn't had a t-bone in, oh, well, longer than I remembered. Too long, anyway. I picked a nice one, dropped it on the grill over the hot charcoal, and listened to the sizzle. The smell coming off the cooking meat was drool provoking. I had forgotten how good some things are that the average person takes for granted until they are put out of his reach. I cooked it until I thought it to be about halfway there, then flipped it. The beauty of the browned steak with the grill marks symmetrically aligned across the surface rivaled anything in the Museum of Art in New York City, or at least at that moment seemed to. It was surpassed only from the fragrance rising from it. The culmination of perfection would come in the devouring of it. I picked up my tray, went by the table, scooped up a large portion of mashed potatoes and poured about a cupful of brown gravy over it. The gravy spread around the beautiful t-bone. A spoonful of green beans, and the plate was sufficiently loaded. On the way to a table, I scooped up a can of Pepsi-Cola out of a cattle trough of ice and water. I sat down, sprinkled a little salt and pepper on the steak and potatoes, cut off a piece, and left this earth and went straight to heaven.

As I sat and slowly relished my meal, I noticed a lot more people coming in and out than the last time I was here. Across the street there was a building with a large rotating radar dish. Occasionally, the sound of a big jet on approach to Tan Son Nhut International Airport would drown out all the other noise around me, sometimes causing the ground under me to shake. It was evident to me that the amount of personnel was being beefed up. I kept to myself, not wanting to start any conversations in which I couldn't explain myself completely.

As the hunger in my body was appeased by the huge meal, my thoughts went to finding Dan or someone else I might know. The folks at Da Nang obviously didn't know what to do with me. I went over to the barber shop and asked for a haircut and shave. I sat down and the young Vietnamese man quickly cropped my already short hair into a neater cut, then laid me back in the chair and wrapped a hot towel round my neck and face. Shortly he was back. He held the straight razor above my face and proceeded to give me a shave. As I watched his face, I realized that I would never truly trust anyone again for the rest of my life. His eyes were impersonal as he stroked my face with the sharp blade. I have to say I was relieved when he laid it aside and wiped my face with the warm towel. He finished with a splash of some sweet smelling aftershave and sat the chair up. I thanked him and paid him. Time for my search to continue.

I took a stroll to the gate and caught a rickshaw to downtown Saigon. I had the driver drop me at the Continental Hotel. I walked down the street, stopping at shops and just looking. When I found a shop whose proprietor spoke English, I would chat with them. I spent the entire afternoon in the world that I had first known when I came to

Vietnam. If I was to stay here, I had to know more about these people. Were they happy with us, being in their country, or were we intruders? I found if I questioned them, they would clam up, almost afraid to talk. Why? Had all the wars in the past created a people that had no trust? No one I ever spoke to showed signs of patriotism. They instead seemed to focus on their family and their livelihood. I dunno, maybe that is a good thing. President Kennedy, from what I had learned at Da Nang, seemed to be starting to pay more attention to what was going on here. Vice President Johnson had recently made a trip over here, praising President Diem. I didn't understand that. He seemed to be a tyrant to me, and not too well-favored among most of the people, especially the Buddhist. I knew little of them, except they seemed quite a peace-loving people. He was supposed to be Christian, but didn't resemble the Christians I had grown up with back home. Or perhaps I was just too young to understand politics at all. I loved my country, I still had a little tingle inside every time the flag was raised.

I could see, though, that we seemed to be in the process of building a military force here. I didn't much like that idea. Men like Lieutenant Tran needed to be stopped, but was this the way to do it? Did we have the ability to correct hundreds, no thousands, of years of cultural thinking and beliefs? I shook my head at my own confusion. I stopped at the little theater on Tu Do Street and took in a movie, the first in a long time. It was an American movie about teenage rock and rollers and street racing. It had been redubbed in Vietnamese, but it didn't matter. It was thought provoking. These were people of my generation. Was I, after all this shit I had waded through, eventually to go back and resume life at the malt shop and the corner garage? What would I talk about? I got up and left about halfway through the movie, my head too full to enjoy the innocence.

It was dark when I got back to the hotel. I picked a table out front and a waiter came and took my order. I ate alone. I felt alone. This place reminded me too much of Silver. It wasn't the rest and relaxation I had thought it would be. His ghost was everywhere, in my every thought. Even the beautiful girls weren't an enjoyment any more. I sat smoking a cigarette. I had reclaimed my Chesterfield

Kings immediately upon reaching civilization again. They were the only medicine I had to numb my thoughts with now.

Eventually the drinking crowd arrived. The second table over from me was occupied by three men, probably in their 30s or early 40s. They had been deep in discussion since their arrival. Soon, they were joined by two more men. I had seen these two at the Embassy before, one of them was CIA. The other, I'm not sure, but probably. I always enjoyed the street life on Tu Do, and I started to relax a bit.

The longer the men drank, the louder they got. One of them was from a chemical company based in America, the other an American steel company, and the third a rubber company, never heard which one. The chemical guy seemed to be the one that was supplying the defoliate that the military was just starting to use so that the VC had no place to hide. I had to chuckle about that. The VC were much smarter than that. You could get rid of every leaf and every blade of grass and the VC would still be a formidable foe.

I listened to them for over an hour, talking about actions that would accelerate the war.

It would be good for business, it would create more jobs in America. I was becoming increasingly agitated and angry. Finally, I called my waiter, paid my check, and flagged a taxi. Was this the way my country did business? Money paid for with blood? It just hurt me to think that. I had not been brought up to think of America that way. Was I raised and taught this innocence in school on purpose? Were we groomed to be sheep, and to not even run from the slaughter?

My taxi dumped me at the gate to Tan Son Nhut. I went to the big hanger and bought me a Pepsi and a Snickers bar and another pack of Chesterfield Kings. I had smoked a bunch today, too much! I picked one of the couches in the lounging area and lay back and closed my eyes. It had been a long day. I awoke to the sounds of reveille. I got up and went to the latrine and washed my face and hands. I went through the mess line and got my breakfast - scrambled eggs, bacon, toast - then picked up another plate and got an order of SOS After I ate, I wandered back into the receiving area where I had met Silver the first time. I stood looking at the chair he had been sitting in. A young airman asked, "Can I help you, Sir?"

I turned and looked at him. "No, I was just looking for a ghost."

He looked at me as I walked out of the room.

I caught another taxi to the Embassy. I walked all over the building looking for Dan. Finally I asked someone, and they pointed me downstairs. I went down a flight of stairs and a hallway and there was Dan. I walked up to his desk.

"I have been looking for you everywhere."

"And we have been looking for you. Where is Silver?"

I was taken aback. "Silver is dead, Dan!"

"Oh my God! How? When?"

"Several weeks now."

"We knew the village had been burned."

I related the events of the last few weeks. I showed him the marks on my arms and back.

"Boots, I am so glad that you have made it."

I thanked him, and asked if he knew what could have happened to Silver's body. He said he would investigate, but guessed the patrol that had his body might have gotten hit again. He related the event about Quinn and Groom and the guys with them that were killed. I told him I was aware of that and had actually seen Quinn and Groom. I told him I was going back to Da Nang and if he had any news to let me know.

I went back to Tan Son Nhut to catch a hop back to Da Nang. The only ride I could get was on a C-119. It was being loaded when I got out to the flight line. It contained a big four-wheel drive Michigan front-loader, pallets of barrels of something, about thirty or so personnel and their gear, and other stuff I didn't bother to identify. They closed up the cargo hold. Everyone got aboard and the pilot taxied out to the flight line. He wound the engines up, and we took off down the runway at a speed so slow that terrified me. I knew we would never get up, but sure enough, about three quarters of the way down he aborted. *Oh good, now he will unload something.* Wrong!! He taxied back, turned around and really cranked it up. We lumbered back down the runway. I was pretty sure this guy had been trained by Air America. When we hit the point of no return I thought *Oh my*

God, this is how it was going to end, but at the end of the runway he pulled it off the ground. We trimmed trees for the first two miles. If there were any VC snipers out there that day taking pot shots at the planes as was their custom, I bet they shit their pants and fell out of the trees!

We finally got altitude and turned north. We had no sooner gotten some altitude when we ran into a storm. I am not kidding you when I say that the lightning was bouncing off the wingtips, and the wingtips were flopping like vulture wings taking off from a feast. We would fall a hundred feet at a time, then shoot right back up. I was never so sick in my entire life.

When we landed I fell out of the plane and into my bunk. I was so sick and so tired. I was not in my right mind. I was not thinking clearly at all. I tossed and turned for some time, thinking about the conversation at the hotel, the loss of Silver's body, the seeming disregard for my capture. Is this the reward for trying to be a good soldier? Not that I was considered one. Then the guilt. My uncle never complained about the winter of '44 at the Bulge. Did my great-grandfather quit mid-war during the Civil War? The answer to both was no! Indeed, my Great-Grandpa Bartlett had been captured and spent thirty months in the terrible Yankee prison camp at Rock Island, Illinois. *Thirty months!* No telling what he went through.

Next morning about 0800, I went to the headquarters building and reported in for assignment. I was assigned to a Lieutenant Lane. I knocked on his door.

"Enter," came the reply.

I walked in and introduced myself as reporting for duty.   The good lieutenant shuffled through a bunch of papers. Finally he acknowledged me with an "At ease."

I watched him as he read some papers. Finally, raising his eyes to look at me he said, "You know, this looks like one of the most preposterous reports I have ever read. I would like to get to the bottom of it. Right now."

"Yes, Sir"

"First, to what unit have you been assigned to while in Vietnam?"

"None, Sir. My orders came from non-military authorities or someone at MAAG-V since my arrival here."

"I'm sorry, things don't work that way. I think you have either deserted or you are AWOL from some unit. Is this your correct name?"

"Yes Sir. Sir, excuse me, Sir, you think I am lying? Sir, you need to call the CIA office at the Embassy in Saigon and talk to Dan. He will confirm me."

"I don't have to call anyone. You can do KP or latrine duties until someone shows up looking for you."

At that, I just saw red. All my anger just burst! I just didn't care anymore! Nothing mattered. He called me a liar, just like that fucking NVA Lieutenant had done!

"Sir, not that I am too good to do any of these duties, I'm not. But you are an idiot! You are too stupid to be in charge of anyone! You are an asshole! I have met good men and soldiers here, and I will not take any orders from a sorry piece of shit like you! Good day, *Sir*!"

I spun on my heel and left the building. I had not gone far, when a jeep pulled up and two MPs jumped out. "You have to go with us."

I looked at them. "Ok."

I was transported to the stockade and put into a cell. Caged again. By my own people. My already thoroughly screwed-up mind dropped through a hole in the world. I walked to a bunk. The anger abated. I lay down, facedown. I would have cried, but it would have taken a passion of some sort, and I had no more. I was at the end. Of what I did not know, but nevertheless, I was at an end.

Food was brought in. I didn't even look at it. I lay facedown. One of my jailers came by.

"Hey, aren't you that guy that escaped from the VC?"

I looked up. "Yeah"

"I thought so. What are you doing here?"

"Some asshole lieutenant, name of Lane, called me a liar, or a deserter. I told him to go fuck himself and walked out of his office."

"Yeah, he's an idiot."

"I tried to get him to get a hold of a CIA operative at the Embassy in Saigon, but he refused."

"What's the guy's name?"

"Dan is all I know him by, redheaded guy."

"No promises, I'll see what I can do."

"Thanks."

I sat on my bunk all night, smoking and thinking. What had I gotten out of my stay here in Vietnam? I had learned to kill people, first off. My heart had been broken, a couple of times. Lost my best friend, been caged and beaten, ran for my life, realized my country sucked after always believing it to be special. I had learned to never trust anyone for any reason, and would never again. I would always be looking for an out, the rest of my life. All I wanted was out, any way possible! And now I was back in a cage.

The days went by slowly. My thoughts became angrier. I wanted to hurt someone. I had never felt that way in my life. I needed some kind of balance, something to lift me out of this place. I slept fitfully that night. Dreams and nightmares plagued my unconscious mind. At some point I met Silver. We walked together in the jungle of the central highlands. We talked about the beauty that was this place and he told me stories of the people who live there. I felt an ease, a comfort, just to see his face again, to feel the comfort of his knowledge and words.

I awoke in the wee hours of the morning before daylight. I knew now what I had gained. I had gained the knowledge of true friendship. In a few short months a stranger had turned me into a person to be reckoned with, a person of capabilities that will again and again save his life in very uncertain circumstances. I can never repay the debt to him. But, I can also never betray his confidence in me.

I was lying awake when reveille was sounded. I was up and doing my exercises when my breakfast arrived. My jailer remarked, "Feeling better?"

I shot him one of Silver's half grins, "Yeah, as long as you guys don't torture me after breakfast."

He looked at me like I was nuts! He wasn't too far from right. I spent the days doing my martial arts and exercises. At one point a couple of the MP's came in and asked me what I was doing. I told them about what Silver had said about the martial arts, and the philosophy behind it.

One of the guys said, "I would like to try it, the movements are great."

I said, "I will be happy to teach you what I know."

"You sure you are not going to kill me and try to escape?"

I laughed. "And where would I go?"

That afternoon they let me out and we went out behind the stockade to what looked like a break area. For about an hour I taught them all that I knew and told them to just practice over and over and over. I told them that, according to Silver, it had to do with your muscles memorizing the moves so that they would just do them without thinking.

We sat on a bench for a while and talked. I was the only one locked up at the time, so it wasn't like they had a lot to do. They asked me about this guy named Silver. That opened up a dialogue that was very dear to me. I told all that I knew, without divulging any real secrets, and that he had been killed.

After that, I got really good treatment, at least for being in jail. They brought me candy bars, soft drinks, cigarettes, and magazines. Others, including the Chaplin, came and visited and talked. Some tried to get me to ask to be released and volunteer for duty. I said I might consider talking to some one, but not that prick Lane. But nothing ever came of it.

I stayed in the Stockade for about two weeks. Late one afternoon I heard a familiar voice out front. In a minute a red head poked through the doorway. "Hey! Boots!"

I came off my bunk like I was sitting on hot coals. "Dan! Oh my God, I have never been so glad to see someone in my life. How did you find me?"

"Long story. Tell me what happened."

I related the circumstances since I had seen him in Saigon. He laughed, "Boy, Silver trained you well, did he not? That is exactly what his reaction would have been, except he would have probably gotten away with it. He had a lot of friends in high places. You have just not been around long enough!"

I nodded. Somehow that was comforting, to think I would have done something that Silver would have done.

"Now, a few days ago, I received a wire that a Senator had the Red Cross looking for a person. It took me a little while to remember that it was your name. They were looking for you about the same time I got a note that a guy named 'Boots' was in the stockade at Da Nang. It seems your dad has been injured. He is alright now, but they need you at home. Give me a day or so, I will get you out of here."

I said, "Oh, fuck. Do you know what is wrong with my dad?"

"No, I don't. But they assured me it was not a life or death situation, that he is at home and doing well. He is just not able to work, and needs your help. So sleep well. I will talk to you tomorrow morning."

Sleep well, my ass. I didn't sleep at all that night. I worried some about my folks. I hadn't written them since my escape. I didn't know if I should tell them. There was no way I could ever talk to them about what I had been doing.

Next morning, before noon, Dan walked in. He looked and me and said, "You should have nailed that asshole. I sure wanted to. What a prick!"

"Yeah, that seems to be the common

feeling everyone around here has. What's up?"

"He won't cooperate. I am seeing the CO of MAC-V in an hour. We will get this done."

My heart sank a bit, but Dan seemed confident. We sat and talked about some of the stuff that had happened in our operations with the Montagnards, and about some of the operations in the highlands going on at the present. Dan was very candid with me, and I appreciated it. When he was there I felt some of my old confidence return. He left shortly. He was gone for two, three hours.

Late in the afternoon, he came in. With him were my two favorite MP's. I can't remember their names, but if you guys read my story and recognize me, thank you again for your kindness in a bad time.

"Boots, you are a free man, for a second time. This is also not going to be on your record. Here are all your papers. Your ID papers, your dog tags, military ID card and passport. Also, we gave you a service record for your time here. It is not what you did, but it will prove you were on active duty for that time period."

I looked at all the documents. I put the passport in my pocket, along with the military ID card, the dog tags around my neck, and shoved the rest back into the manila envelope. I looked up at Dan, "You know what Dan? I had just about forgotten who I was!" He smiled.

Both the MP's shook hands with me and wished me good luck! Dan took me to a waiting jeep, and we rode out to the flight line. A C119 was being unloaded. We sat in the jeep, and I lit up a Chesterfield King.

Dan turned to me, "Boots, it is unfortunate this had to happen to you. You did a fine job. You are a good man, you did your duty. Be proud of what you did. Silver always spoke highly of you. He didn't do that undeservingly. Whatever you do with the rest of your life, I hope the experiences you have had here help you. I say again, I am proud to have known you and worked with you."

I reached out and shook his hand. "Dan, I will never forget you. For sure, you got me into this, and now you got me out of it. Thank you for both. One thing for sure, I will never forget it, for the rest of my life."

I took my bags out of the back and walked

to the plane. I showed my papers to the crew chief and he told me that I had my choices of seats. I walked into the huge empty plane. I saw there was only a half dozen troops with their gear. I sat in a wall seat by a window. The big engines came up. We started our taxi, and very quickly we were airborne, the nose pointed at a setting sun. Quickly we banked to the right.

I looked out over the jungle as the sun dropped below the mountains where so much had happened to me in the past months. I almost, for a moment, felt a pang of homesickness, a sorrow at the parting. Then we were headed out over the South China Sea. I unfastened my belt and walked out and lay down on the belly cargo door. There was a large crack. I looked down and watched the ocean speed by, taking me away to another world that right now seemed foreign and unfamiliar. I felt the irony of the moment, and I remember it well now, fifty some odd years later, that I had come to Vietnam in a loaded plane. And life, while there, had been so full of so many things. And here, now, I leave, and my vehicle is empty. Empty as I felt at that moment!

Chapter 11

I stepped off the little bus into the warm balmy air at my appointment, Clark Air Force Base, PI. I always thought the PI should stand for Paradise Incorporated. I entered the office, signed in at the window, and took a seat in the waiting area. I had only been out of the stockade for a few hours. I was still a bit skeptical of any chance of freedom, but Dan had said, "Boots, you're going home!"

Pretty soon a serious looking man came in and called my name. I lifted my hand and he motioned me to follow him. He took me back to a small room where two more men in suits awaited. I sat down across from them.

"So, Mr. Boots." I looked up, he had smiled briefly. "When you leave this room, that name stays here. That will be over. So, starting at the beginning, from the first day you arrived in Southeast Asia, tell us everything you have been involved in. Every detail, all the way to the events of yesterday afternoon."

I sat back in my chair. Everything, huh? Ok. I started talking. As I talked I watched the shadows crawl across the room. As the sun slowly sank into the west, about three hours later, I said, "Well, that's about it."

The older of the three men, I supposed he was about my father's age, spoke. "Well, son. That is quite a story. It's too bad you are going to have to keep it to yourself. But, for your own comfort, what you have been a part of has been of great benefit for your country, and for the Republic of South Vietnam. And on behalf of both of them, we thank you. The reason you are here is to tell you that your active duty is ended. You are going home. Your family, I understand, has had some difficulty and needs you. They have had the Red Cross looking for you. You weren't very easy to find, and after hearing this, I understand why. So, in closing, I am to tell you that you are not to divulge any of your activities to anyone, at anytime, under penalty of treason to your country. My advice is to go home, rejoin your family and community, and forget any of this ever happened. Any comments?"

I could not have kept from smiling. "Yes, Sir. As for forgetting any of this, I don't know about that. But not talking will be easy. You see, Sir, none of this happened to me. It all happened to a guy named 'Boots' and you just said he no longer exists. Sir, he is dead."

"Son, You are dismissed."

Thirty-six hours for someone like me, you would think, would be a piece of cake. But it wasn't. As the old Super Connie lifted off at Clark AFB and headed for the California coast, my doubts returned. I could see something happening. Plunging into the ocean in a fiery ball, maybe, or a change of mind by some military official at Travis, and being put on the first flight back to Vietnam. All these doubts played through my mind.

I looked down from my window seat as we passed over Guam. *C'mon man, get your head together, it's gonna be all right.* I dozed for a few hours. A slight lurch, an air pocket, woke me up. The young soldier next to me said, "You ok, bud?"

I nodded. "Yeah, why?"

"Ah, you were talking to some guy named Silver. Sounded pretty bad. Where you been?"

"Nowhere in particular. Silver used to be a friend of mine, he got hurt."

"Ok, just curious."

The way he looked at me, I didn't think the curiosity was satisfied. Gotta watch this. No heavy sleep, just doze.

Hours later, the pilot announced we are landing at Wake Island to refuel.

"Be on the ground about an hour. You may disembark, but don't wander."

I looked out the window. Nothing but water. The plane continued its descent. As it came around, there it was. *Oh shit, we are going to land on that? My grandma made bigger quilts than that.* As we circled in, it got a bit bigger, but not much. Then the final approach. I looked out as the wings appeared to be skimming the waves of the Pacific Ocean. My doubts returned. It looked like the Captain had caught a big wave and was surfing us onto Wake Island. Just then, the wreck of a navy landing-craft flashed by. Seconds later we touched the tarmac, and brakes and throttle-back followed immediately. I looked out, I could see waves on the beach ahead! Oh Shit!

We came to a stop, the door opened, and we stepped out onto the only piece of land in a thousand miles. You could see all around it. We walked over to the small air terminal. I bought a couple of snacks and a soft drink, and some chips for later. I walked outside. There was a plaque with the story of the battle that happened here in the 40's during WWII. I thought, *not much signs of it now.*

I sat and smoked a Chesterfield King and thought about it. Would there be signs of the fighting in Vietnam twenty years from now? Or would it be over by then? My thoughts went back to the men at the Continental Hotel and my last night in Saigon. I hoped they would fail. But would they? Have all Americas wars started like this, over greed and aggression? I still believed in Jack Kennedy, but why didn't he stop it? He had seen war.

Someone said, "We're boarding now."

I walked back out to where the twin-tailed aircraft stood waiting. Soon we were speeding down the runway and lifting off. I took my last look westward over the Pacific. I was lost in my own thoughts for hours, staring out the window. I had a new seat partner, an Air Force Tech Sergeant.

My staring out the window was interrupted by, "Hey buddy, you trying to remember all that ocean?"

I turned to meet his gaze, "Naw, just a lotta stuff on my mind."

"You been to Vietnam, haven't you?"

"Yeah, I was there a while."

"What's it like, over there?"

"I suppose it depends on your duty and what you're doing."

"What were you doing?"

I managed to choke out, "Aw, nothing important. Spent some time at the embassy in Saigon"

The guy on his other side said something to him and distracted him. I took the opportunity to lean back and settle into my pillow and close my eyes. Was I going to have to lie about this from now on? But I couldn't. I couldn't ever talk to anyone about my feelings, my pain, my memories. It wasn't fair. For a second my anger flared. A desire to get even with someone, but who? I slept for a long, long time.

I was nudged awake by the stewardess. "Hey, sweetie. We are landing in Hawaii for a couple of hours. Give you a chance to stretch your legs."

I murmured, "Thanks." I grabbed my overnight bag and walked into the terminal. I found the closest bathroom and took care of those duties. I took some wet paper towels into the stall and refreshed myself as much as possible. I then went out and took my shirts off and washed my body. As I stood there washing, an airman walked in.

"Shit, buddy, what happened to your back?"

"Oh, I had a little accident."

"Looks like someone beat you."

"No, just an accident. Where you headed?" I asked, seeking to change the subject.

"Aw, I'm going to Vietnam."

"What are you gonna do there?"

"Oh, I am an air traffic controller."

I had finished shaving by now, and redressed. "Ok pard, good job to have. Good luck."

I turned and walked out, and checked to see when we were to board. They had set the time back another hour, so I asked one of the counter people if there was a restaurant close by. They suggested one, and I went off to find it.

When I walked in, it was only partially filled with people. I went to the counter and ordered a cheeseburger with fries and a strawberry shake. When it arrived I went to a table and proceeded to devour the aforesaid treat. It was totally great. I remember thinking to myself, *I am never going to allow myself to be hungry again.*

I walked out and breathed the warm tropical air. Night had fallen. I lit a Chesterfield King and looked out at the lights. My thoughts went back to my village in the highlands. I allowed my self to voice my thoughts, "I promise you, I will never forget you. I will keep you alive in my memories. And someday, I will tell the world about you. I will never say goodbye!"

"Never say goodbye to who?"

I turned around quickly. I thought I was all alone, but a pretty girl about my age stood behind me. When she saw the tears in my eyes, she grabbed my hand and put her arms around me and hugged me.

"I am so sorry, I didn't mean to eavesdrop!"

It was then I saw the cigarette in her hand. "It's alright," I said.

We talked for awhile. She was heading home to her parents somewhere on the west coast. She had been going to college here. Finally, I had an idea. "I will probably never see you again. I want to tell you a story. I was told I could never tell it to anyone, but if I don't I will just explode. You don't even know my name, can I tell you?"

"After seeing your face and your tears, I would be honored!"

The next hour and a half, I told her everything, as fast as I could. She laughed with me and cried with me, and hugged me during the hard parts. And when I was done, she came and hugged me again and kissed me on the cheek.

"Thank you. I will cherish this for as long as I live. I will tell my children, when I have them, about the young man I met one night in Hawaii who shared his amazing story."

I turned and hugged her one more time and thanked her. I was able to go and get back on the plane, at bit less agitated than before. I will never forget her for listening to me. I think she somehow knew how important it was.

Early the next morning we landed at Travis Air Force Base. I spent all day processing. About four o'clock, I was handed my DD 214 and final pay, plus travel expenses. I took my bag into the bathroom, took my uniform off, and pulled out my jeans and western shirt. I put them on, slipped my belt on - I had to tighten it a couple of notches. The pants felt a bit loose, but really good. I pulled on my Nocona's and looked in the mirror. Then I looked down at my Nocona's again. I laughed at myself. *I guess some boots will never be forgotten.* On the outside was the same guy from some months ago. I picked up my bags, walked out, and boarded the shuttle to San Francisco International.

After a short ride, we arrived. I went in and purchased a ticket for home. This was surreal. The conversation around me was all about movies and music and jobs and school.

Every thing I heard was of such a superficial nature. Don't these people think of anything serious? I watched a TV news show in the terminal. All kind of news, but nothing about Vietnam. It doesn't exist.

I had a six hour wait. I tried to call my folks, but no answer. Well, it was late. I went and sat in the lounge, listening to the chatter around me. I began to sweat. What was I going to do the rest of my life? Be like them? I felt panic move up in my throat. For the first time in days, I was scared again. I calmed myself. I had learned life lessons; lessons most never get to experience. They should help me go anywhere. Yeah, I was free now. I could go anywhere. Where once had stood an innocent young man with dreams for tomorrow, who trusted everyone around him, who had malice for no one, one who delighted in the everyday things, his family, his friends, now stood a young man alone, afraid of his future, not knowing that what the world presented as a painting of its realism, was really a disguise that it used to manipulate its subjects. I had been brought up in the 40's, a time of patriotism and love of country. I had gone forward to serve my country, as people of my generation grew up expecting to do. Now there would be no bands marching down Main Street, no parade with balloons and confetti. I was to come home and to resume life as if nothing had changed. But I had changed. I was not the same, nor would I ever be. My ghosts would haunt me all the rest of my days, my dreams would wake me with tears in my eyes that I would be unable to explain to the one beside me. I would fight battles in my sleep, so that when I awoke, my partner would ask, "Are you alright?" Oh, I know I'm not the only one. Many others have suffered this illness in all wars. We have gone forth with the vision of youth and come home having suffered a total loss of innocence.

EPILOGUE

Like a lot of stories that came out of the Vietnam conflict, many lives were changed. The thing that is different about this one, I believe, is in the time period in which it happened. I don't believe it could have happened in that place even a year or so later in the mid-1960's because things were moving too fast, and changes were too drastic to allow the cast and crew to stand on the stage that they would have had to stand upon, to have played these parts.

We must remember, for this story to be told, all these souls must die again, both friend and foe, or else they will be forgotten forever. They died once in the past and were remembered only as the novel unfolds. And the young man of whom we speak, who has suffered this Loss of Innocence, can never regain it. He will live out his life with these memories etched into the shadows of his existence, ghosts that can choose to come forth at any time, to bring forth a memory of a time of beauty and sweetness, and peace, or a horror to cause one to cringe into their pillow at night, sometime with pain, so real as to cause one to gasp again as one did with the regular pain. If he is your brother, your lover, your father, your husband, your friend, be aware of his need. For his story was born of his desire to serve, be it right or be it wrong. It nevertheless molded him into the vessel that sits before you today.

SUI'S SONG

When I was young, far a-way from home, I met a young girl,__ who sang me a song! As time passed by, you stole my heart I knew not how, we could e - ver part In a land plagued with war, in a land full of strife, You healed my wounds, you gave me my life I had be-come some-one, that I did-n't know, You healed my spi - rit, and made it grow Come wash my hands, Sweet Su-i, Sweet Sui, Come dry my eyes, Sweet Su-i Sweet Sui

In first light of day, you sat by my bed, you washed my hands, you saw me fed,
I would say thanks, for starting my day, then like a bird you'd fly away,
I would sit for hours and listen to you, not a word that was spoken, I ever knew,
Innocent as a child, yet a women full grown, with you came happiness I'd never known. Chorus

A beautiful face, eyes soft but bright, your hair was long and black as the night,
Your body so graceful, a dancer might yearn, but no stage was ever to see you turn,
Our home that we shared was ever so humble, just a little thatched hut, way back in the jungle
But no palace could ever compare, with all the love we had there to share!   Chorus

Our lives were different, from worlds far apart, joined by the beating of our single heart,
Love that was blind, to the reality of our time, just to be together, was what filled our mind.
But then came that day, when I was not there, no one to protect you, your cries filled the air
Your village destroyed, your family died too, I cried over your body, my Sweet, Sweet, Sui.   Chorus

You lay near our home as if waiting for me, I was blinded by tears, I could not see,
Holding your body all broken and torn, and maybe a child, that would never be born.
For hours on end, you lay on my breast, I knew that soon, I must lay you to rest,
With my own hands, I dug you a grave, there was nothing left but our love to save.   Chorus

My life moved on, and has moved on yet, Sweet Sui in the jungle, I'll never forget,
I will always remember forever so long, the beautiful young girl, who sang me a song!

Final Chorus
Come wash my hands, Sweet Sui, Sweet Sui, Come dry my eyes, My Sweet sweet Sui.

273

www.ingramcontent.com/pod-product-compliance
Lightning Source LLC
Chambersburg PA
CBHW071126170626
46809CB00002B/507